ROMANS - GREEKS & TROJAN WAR PARTY

Beryl Screen

Published by Decimax - London

COPYRIGHT

ACKNOWLEDGEMENTS

Thanks go to Dr Richard J Evans, my supervisor of Classical studies at UNISA. A man of exact dates and political arguments relating to Romans and Greeks, yet always with quiet, patient, charm.

To my dear friend, Dr Noushin Farhoumand, who has encouraged me along the way, to start writing this book, and stop collecting never-ending information.

Karen and John Phillips who enjoy discussing ancient Romans and Greeks, and my daughter Pam Woolford, who have all given me support.

Finally, my grateful thanks and appreciation goes to my son Andrew Screen who has motivated me to study philosophy, art, artefacts, and literature, and who is taking this book to its completed stage.

THE AUTHOR

Beryl Screen has a Master's degree in Classics and a degree in History of Art, from UNISA, and has spent most of her life living in Africa, during which time she painted portraits or other works of art. After hours of work writing about Roman emperors and wars, that were never completed - the author decided to change to writing Roman and Greek humour, or satire. The story is a mixture of allusions and illusions for people of all levels with interests in light-hearted Roman and Greek history. The author now lives in England.

INTRODUCTION

The central theme is the art of deception, imagination and illusion in the year CE 221. Roman friends are drawn humorously together in their daily lives when trading in wines or artefacts, travelling to Capri or attending the Circus Maximus.

They are invited to a weekend party where they have to participate in a condensed re-enacting of the Trojan War, which takes them into Homer's Greek mythical world and their Roman friendships being put to the test.

It is at a time when the emperor, young Elagabalus, became ruler of the Roman Empire. One of the questions raised is whether his grandmother pulled off a hoax, to obtain the highest position of power for herself, and her grandson being a stepping-stone to achieve her goal.

Young Elagabalus gave the Romans much concern when he showed more interest in his god Elagabaal, acquiring several wives, a husband and male lover.

ROMANS - GREEKS & TROJAN WAR PARTY

CHAPTER ONE

Roman friendships and surpriscs

Crossing the road early in the morning requires nimble footwork, as Julia tries to avoid the remains of horse manure that had soiled the street during the night.

Local citizens suffer the displeasure of animal manure when crossing streets. Some residents living in upper apartments often throw rubbish down onto the streets and pavements, even though this is prohibited, adding to the road-cleaning problem.

Horses are allowed into the city at night, and the wealthy like to be noticed as they pass by in their decorative horse-drawn carriages.

It is during these hours of darkness that wagons, pulled by donkeys or horses, provide deliveries or removals of goods to shops, and haulage of building materials, as well as other goods, which keep the city functioning.

Teenage youths, spoilt sons of aristocrats, take pleasure in racing their chariots at night along the paved streets of Rome, causing pedestrians who cross the roads to jump for cover, providing much jeering and laughter from the youths.

City guards are disinterested in these dangerous pursuits. It is easier, in their opinion, for a walker to quickly swivel his head and check at intersections for oncoming traffic, even when chariots are speeding, than for a guard to challenge a consul or senator, about his son's behaviour.

If any punishment were to be given for a youth's behaviour, it would be doled out to the tutor or slave, who had allowed one of their charges to carry out such misconduct. So, bad behaviour continues without any impunity.

It is now early morning and there has been light rain prior to Julia's arrival in the centre of the city. Local street cleaners are hit-and-miss with their cleaning operations, and manure from the previous night is still lodged between the paving, making the slabs slippery.

Julia makes her way to her showroom, carrying in her hand a scroll of designs, being garden layout plans, requested by her new customer Sextus, for a central feature, to be situated near his large garden pond.

Whilst attempting to take a long stride to reach a small dry patch of granite pavement, her elbow is nudged. To gain balance, her hand holding onto the important design sketches loses its grip on the papyrus scroll, which falls onto the wet ground.

Turning to pick up her drawings, she notices a man in his mid-thirties, with dark hair, dressed as a workman, yet he does not look like one. He wears a short tunic and sandals of good quality leather, with an embossed pattern of a ship on the central strap.

She gives the man a glare.

Pointing to a stool, he says, 'A splinter from the stool went into my thumb – sorry I nudged you.'

He gazes straight into her eyes, and gestures with palms outwards and upwards, and with a shrug of his shoulders. He has a slightly apologetic smile – 'Let me pick up your scroll.'

Julia does not find it a smiling matter. Earlier in the morning she had to speak with her father about the progress of her business. Which had slowed in growth and income. Now the designs for her new customer are ruined.

He can see that she is not happy. 'I'm very sorry, but if there's anything I can do to help, I'll gladly make it up to you.'

The scroll is now crumpled, wet, and barely readable.

Momentarily, he places one hand on her elbow – as a kindly gesture to help her balance.

'I'm in your debt, and ...'

Before he can finish she snaps back. 'Don't touch me!' She pronounces the letter 't' as if the sound has suddenly come from a hissing snake.

Even the scrolled papers begin to unravel. The green ribbon that had tied them together, takes on the appearance of a slithery green viper.

She asks him, 'Why are you sticking up posters outside my design showroom?'

'Papinus, whose name you can see on this poster, is going to give a humorous recitation of poems written by the Roman satirist, Juvenal. Would you like to attend? Perhaps bring a guest? It's all free you know – well, I suppose everyone knows that, but I can find you special seats.'

Attracting an audience to a theatre is difficult, especially when competing with events run on the same days such as chariot racing and gladiatorial contests at the Colosseum amphitheatre.

The poster looks colourful and great – but she is not going to say so.

She appears very annoyed. He becomes worried in case she seeks legal advice and claims damages for her ruined work. He is working under an assumed identity – at least until the end of the year.

'Are you an actor?' she asks.

'No, I am part of the management of a theatre and am painting the scenery.'

'Your offer, to make amends for my loss of drawings, is a good suggestion. I will take you up on that … you can look at these soiled sketches, and work with my assistant Lucy to come up with fresh ones. Then you can attend a meeting in an hour's time, and help her explain the drawings to a very important customer.'

'Glad I can be of help.'

'And look smart. Make sure you return here sharply.'

'Who is the customer?'

'I doubt that you know him – he is extremely wealthy. His name is Sextus.'

'Can't wait to see the place,' he knows it is a lie.

She scrutinizes him with semi-closed eyes – as she looks, he pretends to drop the drawings. She was about to yell out, then realises that he is doing it for fun. As she turns away, she has a slight smile at his naughty antics.

Upon departing, she says, 'I have a meeting with the emperor, Elagabalus. I will meet you at Sextus' house later.'

*

Marcus already knows Julia's wealthy client, Sextus. He has lived with his uncle Sextus ever since he was a baby, when Sextus legally made him his son and heir. His parents had died in a shipping accident when they were returning to Italy by sea from Egypt.

Sextus is now suffering from poor health, and at the end of the year is handing over all his wine importing and exporting business, and ownership of a small theatre, to Marcus.

He insisted upon Marcus going to all the countries where they have warehouses, workers, merchants, and ports, as well as visiting vineyards – so that he can understand the profit and loss in each area. Marcus was to go undercover as a lower paid employee to certain places, to identify any improvements which can be made to their business. He grew a short beard and longer hair to make himself less recognisable.

The request for new garden additions arouses Marcus' curiosity. Sextus has shown no interest in the property in recent years. He begins to think that Sextus' new interest in the garden is more to do with two charming ladies, Julia and Lucy, coming to his house, and the garden being an excuse.

Hastily he sends a message to Sextus, saying that he will be arriving with Lucy, who is Julia's assistant. 'I will be in the role of a gopher. Please tell your staff not to show any recognition or mention that I am your family. The two women believe that I am an employee at the theatre.'

Sextus made up his mind to enjoy every moment of his life, as long as his semi-good health lasts. He had worked long hours for many years, but now spends his days trying to re-capture the joys of earlier times, appreciating the pleasures of simple things. His latest interest being the large area around his pond in the garden that had grown into disuse.

Whilst Marcus makes himself respectable before meeting Julia and Lucy at the showroom, his thoughts turn to feisty Julia. He could not remember meeting any other women quite like her – most were friendly and not ready to attack like a lioness.

He began to think about the story of Pygmalion, an ancient sculptor in Cyprus who could not find a perfect woman, because the goddess *Aphrodite* had made the local women repulsive. Pygmalion carved a beautiful female marble statue, and allowed himself to be deceived by his own creativity. So much in love with his own work that he touched, kissed and caressed his art as if it had come to life. But it never spoke or responded to his words or kisses. Pygmalion sought help from the goddess *Aphrodite* – but Marcus stopped thinking about Pygmalion – and instead his thoughts were drawn towards his earlier meeting with Julia.

She caught his attention with her tanned skin and dark eyes and hair, but it was the slight smile on her face as she moved away from him, when he teased her, which caught his interest. He realises that she can change from being fiery then showing a sense of humour, and this attracted him.

If he can create some good plans for the pond at the house, then perhaps he can spend more time with her.

His thoughts went back in time to other women who briefly attracted his attention. One was Anna, a Scottish woman who lives in London, and the other was a quiet and reserved young woman, Samara, who lives in Arles, France.

Marcus met Samara and her parents when they were travelling on a barge up the Rhône River, from Marseilles to Arles.

Marcus had planned upon arrival, to stay a night at a tavern in Arles, then after a short break, continue with his journey to meet with owners of a vineyard twenty-five miles east of Arles.

He was looking forward to the evening at his favourite tavern in Arles, where he had stopped on previous occasions, and always enjoyed their vegetable-filled soup and a portion of roast boar pie.

Whilst on the barge, the parents of Samara requested Marcus to join them at their chateau for a night or two, before continuing to his destination.

Their family chateau appeared quite splendid from the outside as they approached it from the road, leading towards a narrow dirt track, and then a small bridge.

They crossed over the quaint bridge that spanned an old moat beneath, and then came to the entrance of the chateau.

But, once across the threshold and through a large wooden arched double-door, the interior was disappointingly dilapidated.

Samara and her mother made their way upstairs, whilst the host went to speak with the servants.

Wandering around, Marcus notices that in some of the entertainment rooms and entrance hall, the walls have collections of spears or javelins and other weapons displayed in fan-like patterns. Or displays of weapons arranged to go up the walls, as if rungs of ladders.

The spears were of different lengths. These weapons provided the military greater ability when aiming at men or horses charging in battle.

He touched a *pilum* and found it to be extremely sharp with a barbed end. It would seem practically impossible to dislodge it, should it pierce a chest shield, or the body or legs of an animal or a man. He shudders at the thought.

On the wall are three-dimensional facial masks made of beaten gold, bronze or silver.

Each mask depicts the image, *imago,* of an emperor and is held high on a staff or pole by the leading cohort in honour of the emperor who had formed that particular legion.

Emperor Septimius Severus had formed three legions, but Marcus could not see this emperor's mask shown on the wall. Septimius Severus had been the uncle of the present emperor Elagabalus.

At that moment the host, Decimus, joins him.

'I think you will enjoy looking at this other wall. I served with a legion many years ago but was wounded, causing a knee injury. Since then I buy and sell old military weapons to collectors in many countries.'

As they approach, Marcus sees a display of very early military standards showing animals, such as a horse, eagle, wolf, or boar. Also, standards from an even earlier time of the Roman Republic depicting a Minotaur.

'You will see, on this next collection, that four-footed animals are no longer displayed on standards. It is still the time of the Roman Republic, but now you can see that there is the eagle, Aquila. This particular item is well over three hundred years old.'

Obviously, the host had taken some years to collect these artefacts.

Marcus wondered whether military men entering the rooms and seeing the spears on display, could find some secret war strategy, or signalling messages of pincer movements by using the wall patterns and designs. Or perhaps it was just the owner trying to fill the walls and hide any cracks.

He imagined conversations with guests being very amicable with the host knowing he was in the seat of power, surrounded by all his weapons. Just a leap at the wall, then a quick grab, allowed him to be fully armed. Perhaps a warning, to any competitor guest, that the host should always be allowed to win any argument.

Better to keep the conversation low-key and talk of food and travel.

Cousins, aunts and uncles now join them at the chateau. The family barely leave him alone. When he speaks with Samara, a chaperone replies. She seems only allowed to sit and be present, as if part of a display, like the wall display.

It reminded him of reading about the ancient Greek Olympiad where two artists painted reality. Zeuxis painted grapes so real that even the birds flew to the painting as if they could be eaten. Parrhasius had painted a curtain so lifelike that Zeuxis asked him to open the curtain to see what it revealed.

Did the family make Samara their life-like curtain, he wondered? A woman looking real – yet in reality, unable to reveal her inner thoughts or true presence.

He wanted to invite her to join him the following day, to visit the Arles' theatre and amphitheatre – which he had heard about, but never seen. There was no public event on that day. He just wanted to look at its Roman construction so that he could tell his uncle, or better still buy a street artist's painting to take back to Sextus.

In the afternoon, Samara had been in her bedroom resting or perhaps sewing. Marcus needed to have a private word to see if she liked the idea, and ask her, hopefully, to bring with her no more than one chaperone.

It was difficult with the 'cohort' family around, to discover what her personal opinion might be on such an invitation.

He knocked gently on her door.

A noise nearby seemed to indicate that she had replied. He thought she said 'enter'.

Walking straight into her boudoir he saw two people on a bed.

Who was this naked man – this exposed hairy bottom – on top of his new girlfriend? He hardly knew the woman and now he felt confronted by a French cuckold situation.

Was he ready to defend his honour?

Wrong room he realised ... but ... too late to proffer an excuse. It was no cuckold predicament that his imagination had allowed him to invent. Her parents were having sex. But now he had the image of her father's rear end, still set in his mind.

Walking straight out seemed rude. Shaking hands upon departure was not a gesture to be entered into.

He muttered something – speechless for a moment.

The father shouted at him. 'You,' and he paused, 'Italian people are all the same – wanting to look at others having sex'.

What did the father mean by this remark!

Romans were not known to be voyeurs. They are men of action.

Scribbling a brief note, he left it on the entrance hall table – beneath another display of the dreaded weaponry. He collected his belongings and quickly departed. Not wishing to experience an old *pilum* or barbed spear piercing his behind.

The other woman in his life was Anna, a young Scottish woman, living in London with her brother Rufus.

She had strikingly blue eyes and orange-red hair, which she simply tied back with ribbons. Rufus, her brother, exported metalwork, such as lamps and door locks. Anna looked after the creative side of the business, and enjoyed designing jewellery and broaches. Marcus, when they became business friends, agreed that Anna and Rufus could use some storage area in his warehouse at the London docks for their goods awaiting export.

Anna was arty and enjoyed telling Celtic stories, and with friends used to act out scenes to audiences in the villages around where she lived. Marcus had a close friendship with Anna. They still keep in touch.

He remembered one fond moment when she taunted him with the remark: 'Salve, pulcher Marcus ... Hello handsome Marcus.'

He laughed. 'Every time we meet, you come up with a different greeting – are you trying to improve on your Latin?'

'Yes. I seem to speak simple Latin. You use more expressive words. However, I must say – I love your accent.'

'What accent! I am man of Rome with a perfect accent … not one from the provinces!'

They had an ease and familiarity where they could tease each other.

In Scotland she would speak Gallic. In London she would speak in simple Latin, and rolling her 'r' sounded slightly different to how the Romans would sound the letter. He liked listening to the way she pronounced the letter 'r' which sounded like a trilling bird.

He had invited her to Rome, for a holiday. But she said that she did not like to travel so far.

'What – not even to look at Rome's Forum, the shops with traders from all around the Roman world, as well as it's places of entertainment?'

When he left London, they agreed to keep in touch, even though the mail took a long time. She told him, 'I will have a little bird imprinted on my letter seal. So that when you see the seal on the outside you will know it is from me.'

Marcus replied, 'I will have two olive leaves on mine, one for you and one for me when we next meet.'

Over time her letters would arrive with a letter seal showing one bird with its mouth open as if squawking. Perhaps hinting that he owed her a letter.

So much for memories relating to the women in his life.

*

Cause and Effect

In preparation of meeting Lucy at the showroom and travelling with her to the appointment with Sextus, he visited his long-haired and bearded barber. Marcus reckoned the man received his training many years earlier in the legion. He cut and chopped, with great speed, as if a thousand soldiers were waiting in a queue.

But in reality, after Marcus' treatment, the only remaining customer was a teenage boy drawing a gladiator on his wax tablet with a pointed stylus.

The barber was now extremely wealthy, owning two shops, a house and small farm. Customers either provide him with good financial tips, or perhaps customers gave the barber large tips, with the hope that the skilled knife-held hands will stay steady when shaving chins and throats.

Give a good tip or be on your guard at your next visit. It was always good, he thought, to check in the mirror after completion and find one's neck is still intact. A relief! No small sticky pieces of papyrus!

After changing into suitable clothing, Marcus makes his way to the showroom to meet up with Lucy.

His journey is in a covered carriage, (*a litter*), supported on poles with two bearers lifting the weight of the poles in the front, and two bearers supporting the weight at the back. Upon arrival at the showroom, they are told to wait for him and Lucy.

During his absence, Lucy had been applying her make-up. Ndio, a slave, brushed Lucy's blonde hair, braided it, and formed a few curls on the top of her head to make her seem taller.

Ndio knew little about her childhood prior to becoming a slave. She remembered being separated from her mother who was taken away with many others on a boat. She then attached herself to other young people whom she did not know, but learned that they were all in the hands of slave traders. They all just followed instructions.

The next thing she remembered was looking at the bottom of her foot and noticing that white chalk was on it. She was being sold at a slave auction. A card was hung around her neck. Not far from where she was standing she could see large buildings and heard people saying that they were in Rome.

People at the auction were looking at her. In the crowd was a tall, blonde man with a kindly face. She had seen others being bought and taken away by ugly people, so she hoped that this man would buy her.

Gundher asked in Latin: 'What is your name'.

She did not understand the language he spoke and thought he said – do you want to come with me. She replied 'Ndio' which means 'Yes' in her own language from Africa.

After that she became known as Ndio.

Gundher gave her a cloak and took her to the house where the other household slaves washed her and gave her clothes. She was told that her job was to play with Julia, the daughter of the patriarch, senator Quintus. Her work included keeping Julia's room tidy, playing ball, and lots of other things, bathing, and seeing that she eats her food, Julia was five years younger.

As Julia grew older, Ndio learned Latin with her, reading and writing, and realised that one day she could buy her freedom, *manumission*, like Gundher. She did not understand that emperors had placed a *manumission* tax upon any owner of a slave who wished to provide a loyal slave with freedom. This limited the owner from providing too many slaves with freedom.

Now, no longer a child, she is still living in the same place, but the senator has given her permission to work in the showroom of Julia's new business, where she earns a small amount of pay.

Lucy, Julia's cousin, moved to Rome from her parent's farm in southern France, and shares Julia's small house in the grounds of the senator's town mansion.

When Sextus, whom Julia called her 'wealthy customer', first paid a visit to the showroom, Ndio noticed that he constantly gazed at Lucy and Julia, and she did not trust him.

Ndio was unaware that he was slowly dying of old age and a weak heart – and just wanted to find happiness in his remaining years and enjoy the company of young people who had zest, energy and excitement for even the smallest things of life. Finding new plants, taking an interest in birds, insects and wild animals.

He wanted to distract his thoughts from his deteriorating body, and sought to find the joy and pleasures he experienced many years ago. He had worked hard to build up his business, and had found it difficult in those years to relax. Now he was preparing to retire and find other interests.

Unfortunately, Sextus' efforts to act younger makes him appear eccentric. He had dyed black his somewhat grey hair and stuck on the top of his bare patch a small hairpiece, thinking nobody would notice. Slight colouring on his face is to hide his sallow skin. He keeps his eyebrows and beard neatly trimmed beard, and nails polished. Sextus swings a black ebony walking stick with an ivory and gold handle, to give the appearance of being debonair, but really to aid his balance.

Ndio, when she first saw him, thought his appearance was very suspect. As she put the finishing touches to Lucy's hair, she places a blue sapphire hairpin on the top.

Looking at herself in a hand-held mirror, Lucy says, 'I do not want the hair pin.'

'It is for your own protection. If Sextus gets too difficult to handle, then slide out the sapphire and beneath it is a small red pill. Put it in his drink and he will collapse for around three hours. This will give you time to leave.'

Lucy just left it in her hair to keep Ndio happy.

Julia greets Marcus when he arrives at the showroom, with his scroll of roughly copied sketches, and looking less like a workman. She was supposed to have left to meet Elagabalus, but had been kept busy on the drawings for his pond.

She instructs Marcus, 'You must only speak if Sextus, the customer, requires further explanations. Otherwise leave everything to Lucy. As soon as my meeting with Elagabalus is finished I will join you both.'

Marcus was not in agreement with Julia's drawings showing statues of nymphs scattered in various parts around the trees and grounds.

The business and all the property will come under the control of Marcus at the end of the year. He prefers a design that both Sextus and he can live with and enjoy. Probably, Julia is just following Sextus' orders.

'What's in it for me if I get your new customer to request more additional work?'

'Nothing. Remember, you ruined my initial drawings. But, Lucy and I may invite you to eat with us,' she says jokingly.

'Then I'd better work hard – I hope you will have good things to eat.'

'If you bring in more work, we may bake a good loaf of herb bread!'

'Hope you will also offer something sweet to go on it – like honey!'

Their good banter was interrupted by the arrival of a litter, which had gold trimmings and embroidered curtains, and the outside painted red and gold. It belongs to Sextus, who is supposed to be waiting in his house, and not appearing at the showroom.

Lucy is quite impressed with the carriage. She makes her way towards Sextus – she does not even give Marcus a backward glance when she steps into the carriage and the door is closed.

Sextus gives Marcus a wave and a winning grin, as if they were in competition. The front-runner of the vehicle clears pedestrians out of the way as the carriage departs.

Lucy sits on the silk covered seating which has been stuffed with soft duck-down feathers. She notices the heavily embossed embroidery and expensive furnishing. When the carriage is on the move, the runners begin to trot with a slight swaying movement, and she has difficulty keeping her feet on the floor. She is not tall, and can only sit on the edge of the seating.

The runners had worked for Sextus many years and know his routine. They take off at speed, rocking the carriage from side to side, allowing their employer to become overly protective towards the young attractive lady who grabs hold of him for support. He places his arm on her shoulder for a few minutes or briefly holds her hand in a protective manner.

He would have liked to let his hand slip from resting occasionally on her shoulder to her breast, but he knows that in his old age this is not acceptable. Strange, he thought, how old age does not prevent him from having an imaginative memory.

After a few slips and slides, Lucy tries to open the curtains and tells him that the jogging is making her feel sick.

He is forced to stop the carriage.

At this point, Marcus catches up and shakes his head at Sextus for his unacceptable behaviour.

Sextus overtakes him again.

Marcus sits in his smaller and less impressive litter with no front-runner to clear the way ahead. They are constantly held up at busy intersections or near shops, whilst people slowly cross roads, talking with friends.

Ndio sits in the litter with him. Her small figure perched upright on the edge of the seat with her peach-coloured umbrella, neatly closed, and placed upright on the floor and held between clasped hands.

'What work is Julia doing for the emperor?'

'He has asked for some ideas or designs for a water feature and a statue. Julia hopes that this order will lead to other orders from the emperor's friends,' replies Ndio.

Marcus' thoughts then moved to Elagabalus, who became emperor at fourteen years of age. Now three years older, the young man has not made a good choice of friends. It is widely known, that he mixes with sycophants or freeloaders who take advantage of him.

Prior to his arrival in Rome, he lived in Emessa, Syria, acting as High Priest at the local temple, attended by worshippers of the god Elagabaal.

His god, in the form of a meteorite or baetyl, is believed by worshippers to have come down from the sun in the form of a messenger. There are several meteorites at places in the Near East, which are held in great respect, yet not all worshippers are supporters of the god Elagabaal.

Marcus wonders how Julia, whose main business interests relate to the selling of statues of ancient Greek gods, many shaped like humans, will be of interest to Elagabalus, whose own god is abstract in form.

Ndio interrupts his thoughts. 'Oh, it looks like we're here!'

*

Mist, water and *Diana (Artemis)*
Lucy is accompanying Sextus in the garden when Marcus and Ndio arrive. They discuss the designs, as suggested by Julia.

Ndio walks closely behind Lucy, holding the umbrella to keep the sun off Lucy's head, but also to stay close enough to listen into the conversation.

Marcus wanders off towards the large pond where cypress trees and conifers surround the water. The ground is a little higher on one side where trees are more plentiful. On the opposite side of the pond, there are fewer trees, where rays of sunlight creep through the branches, creating a feeling of mystery.

Eventually the others join him, and approve of the spot chosen by Marcus for a water feature.

'May I make some suggestions,' he says, without waiting for a reply.

'I think on the other side of the pond, where there is intermittent sunlight, will be a good place for a statue of the beautiful goddess *Diana*. A carving made with the best translucent white marble. Surrounding *Diana* there could be sculptures of her nymphs by her side.'

'The carving, of the goddess *Diana,* needs to be carried out by specialist artisans using marble imported from a good region in Greece.'

'I have heard that the best artisans use a special saw for such good quality marble, and they also use fine sand from Ethiopia and India. It is this fine sanding that provides the smooth texture which people like to feel when they slide their hands over the surface.'

Sextus agrees to use only the best carvers and material. The touch of smooth marble, and its finely carved workmanship and beauty appeal to him.

Marcus continues with the imagery. 'The statue of the semi-naked *Diana* should be positioned close to the water's edge. The story is told that upon hearing a sound on the opposite bank, *Diana* stands up to leave, whilst her nymphs attempt to wrap a thin translucent robe to cover her waist.

'The nymphs, semi-naked, with translucent skirts clinging to their wet bodies, should be made from a lesser quality marble than that for *Diana*. Making the onlooker drawn more towards the vision of the beautiful *Diana*. A vision in a spinney.'

Everyone agrees – even Ndio nods her head in unison. Then she asks, 'What is a spinney?'

'It's a group of trees surrounding a pond.'

'I am sure you all know the story of *Diana* and *Acteon*. But I will remind you.' At this point Marcus was really enthusiastic and had forgotten Julia's warning about only keeping to her plans.

But before Marcus could remind everyone about the story, Sextus gathers everyone around him.

'I slightly remember the story,' said Sextus. It is at tale written two hundred years ago by the Roman writer Ovid – one of his *Metamorphoses*' stories.

'*Diana* - known to the ancient Greeks as the goddess *Artemis*, is bathing in a pond with her nymphs, when a noise from the opposite bank disturbs her. On the opposite side of the pond, where there was less sunlight but more trees, stood *Acteon*, a demi-god.

'He had been hunting with friends and his many hunting dogs, whom he had lovingly given each hound a name. But he grew tired from hunting and left the group, whereupon he came to rest by the trees. He saw *Diana* and gazed across at the beauty of the goddess.

'*Diana* saw him looking at her and rose from the water.

'The nymphs tried to protect their goddess from *Acteon*'s gaze.

'Upon moving away, Diana flicked water at him.

'Sprays or mists of water, touched *Acteon*, causing him to change into a stag. As he stands bewildered, calling out to his friends for help, he notices that his voice is changing into the crying sound of a stag. He realises that he had lost his ability to speak.

'His hunter friends, hearing a stag's cries, go in search of the animal. They do not recognise him. Even his favourite dogs could not see their master.

They only recognise a stag. His cries of help did not prevent the attack – his excited hounds, as well as his hunting friends, quickly go into action for the kill.'

Everyone stood momentarily quiet.

Sextus jokingly said, 'I'll just have to stick up a notice – 'No Water Splashing.'

'We could have a few wooden carvings of stags and small deers in different areas around the trees, making it an interesting walk. With two or three marble seats and a table facing the pond. Perhaps we could also put in some fish, and I am sure that the birds will come,' said Marcus.

He thought it would be a pleasant spot in the garden for his uncle to sit and meditate, or be joined by friends.

'Hopefully you will start the project soon – then I can enjoy your delightful company,' said Sextus looking at Lucy.

'Oh, I should like that.' She was a diffident person and unsure of herself, and would use 'should and could' hoping that she did not offend anyone.

Walking towards Sextus' large house, she chats to him about Roman writers, such as Ovid and his writing of the *Metamorphoses* tales.

'There are some scrolls in my study and you are welcome to come and visit at any time to read or borrow them.' He began to feel like a mentor to this young woman.

He leaves her alone in his study and she looks at books made of velum, and scrolls. Then she sees a box of pictures showing men with prostitutes in various sexual positions and pictures of Priapus with a very enlarged ... just then Sextus returns, and she quickly places the pictures back in the box.

'Oh, my dear, these pictures are for my male customers who come for wine tasting – not for your pretty eyes. Come, let us go and join the others in the dining area.'

They walk through one small dining area with three couches, with very large cream coloured cushions. Low tables with gold detailing are situated in front of the couches for guests to take food and drink.

Proceeding further, they arrive at a much larger room that looks out onto the garden, with fountains and a pool. This room has a very long table with twelve dining chairs facing towards the garden which is surrounded with an abundance of plants, statues and large flowering plants. There are marble paving slabs outside the dining area, which allows for entertainment to take place. Lamps are placed in chosen positions around the garden.

*

Sitting near the end of the dining table

Marcus walks back to the house which he and Sextus share. His thoughts are with Julia, and hoping that she will find time to leave Elagabalus and join them.

An invited guest Papinus, whose name appears on the poster near the showroom when Marcus bumped into Julia, joins Marcus.

'I have seen Lucy here, but where is Julia?' asks Papinus,

'She has an appointment with Elagabalus who wants a fountain and one or two statues around it.'

'I remember in mid-218 when the news reached us in Rome about the demise of the emperor Macrinus, who had replaced emperor Caracalla. Elagabalus' grandmother, Maesa, had told the legions based near to Emessa, that Elagabalus was really the son of the recently assassinated emperor Caracalla. His mother, Soaemias, was supposed to have had had intercourse with her cousin Caracalla,' comments Papinus.

'This must have come as a big surprise to the young teenager, so soon after the death of his real father Marcellus,' remarks Marcus.

Papinus continues, 'Elagabalus looks nothing like Caracalla, who had a strong jawline, and a square-shaped face, always with a central frown on his forehead. Whereas Elagabalus has an effeminate, smooth girlish face and pointed chin – there is no similarity.

'Emperor Caracalla, was the son of emperor Septimius Severus. Both father and son were held in high esteem by the legions. Elagabalus' grandmother played on this closeness of the two emperors to the legions. She created the illusion of Elagabalus being entitled to become hereditary emperor.

'Before he was assassinated, Caracalla had shown concern that there was a plot to kill him, but was unaware that his Prefect of the Praetorian Guard, Macrinus, whose duty was to protect the emperor, was part of the conspiracy.

'The assassination took place whilst Caracalla was in the process of privately adjusting his clothing to attend to his ablutions. For the sake of privacy, his loyal legions, who are not part of the emperor's palace guards, had left him alone.

It was a quick assassination by a man who had been connected with the Praetorian Guard, and the emperor's loyal legions could not save him. Not long after, Macrinus became the next emperor, but Elagabalus' grandmother wanted the legions to remove him.'

Papinus and Marcus arrive at the dining area where they are shown to their seating. They notice that they have been given a place at the end of the table, which means that they will be served poorer quality of food, bread and wine, as is the Roman custom.

*

Quietly at the showroom, Julia thinks about her meeting earlier in the morning with her father, on the terrace at his mansion. She recalls making her way across the grounds from her smaller house on the property to the terrace.

The Italian Mediterranean sun was slowly breaking through after the early morning rain. Servants had brought her some hot bread rolls and honey, and a warm fruit drink.

Watering the plants in front of the house, situated in the fashionable area of Esquiline Hill, is the elderly family gardener. Regardless of sun or rain, he waters every day. It was part of his daily ritual. He has become rather absent minded in his old age and sometimes pulls up the plants, leaving the weeds. Everyone likes him and nobody has the heart to interfere with his routine.

He has been with the family all his adult life. Walking towards the table he presents her with a tiny yellow flower. Julia smiles and thanks him. He used to be head gardener, but now his working area is restricted to the main house.

She is just about to eat when her father, Quintus, walks towards her across the garden. He wears a toga with a broad purple stripe, which only shows the purple when the material flows down from being across his shoulder and then resting across his left arm. He does not like the excessive material across his arm as he is left-handed and it stops his easy movement.

He has a propensity to take things from the table with the left hand, and this causes problems with those using their right hand that sit on Quintus' left side – both attempting to pick up the same goblet.

It is a working day for him, and his mornings are usually very busy, as clients often wait for him at the atrium of the house to discuss business, or accompany him on his way to the Forum. But today he needs to find a few moments with his daughter before meeting his friend, the consul, to travel together to Capitoline Hill.

His friend is always known as 'the consul', even though he has not been a consul recently – however, he is hoping soon to be given another position in one of the provinces, hopefully close to Rome.

Julia's father makes his way towards where she sits on the terrace. He holds his body very erect for a fifty-eight-year-old man. Dignified in appearance, with silver-grey flecks of hair to the sides of his head, and his dark brown hair now growing a little grey in places. He is slim, and has a straight nose, and kindly eyes. His foot-ware is of best quality leather. He gives her a peck on both cheeks.

'Morning, Pater.' It was a name of familiarity she gave to her father from the time she became a teenager.

As he began to take something to eat, she notices that the corners of the tablecloth and napkins have tiny embroidered bees. Could this be an impending sweet discussion! Or – a warning? A sting in the tail!

Pater likes to keep an eye on his daughter's new business. Her finances came from an inheritance following the deaths of her mother and grandmother. Her father encourages Julia's efforts to create her own business, but does not want her to forget that she needs to make a profit to succeed in business.

Julia's uncle, her father's brother, temporarily gave Julia the use one of his new double-fronted shops. The conditions are that when her business is successful that she will pay rent and take out a lease.

'Tell me – how is the business coming along?'

'Well I have a very wealthy client, Sextus. I don't know whether you have met him.'

'We are old friends,' he replies. He is always reluctant to talk about people with whom he is acquainted. Some people like to name-drop. He prefers to hear what the other person has to say first, and find out whether there is equal ground before conversing further.

'Sextus wants ideas to improve the appearance of a section of his garden that is situated by a pond, as well as introduce some ornamental features.

This should bring us in some good business,' says Julia.

'And profit I hope,' he adds.

'Are you going to take Lucy with you?'

'No, Lucy will take Ndio along. I will join them later. After leaving you, I have an appointment with the emperor, Elagabalus. He wants me to give him some rough sketches for statues and a water feature.'

The senator decides not to discuss his personal thoughts about Elagabalus. He must trust that she has enough awareness to act wisely.

Without telling Julia about his cause for alarm, he breaks the silence. 'I want you to take Gundher with you.'

'Yes, I was thinking of doing that. Gundher will be able to use his association with the craftsmen's guilds, and his knowledge of marble.'

'I'm sure I can handle the young emperor, and get him to buy the statues and create a beautiful pond.'

Walking towards the courtyard with her father he said, 'I really must be on my way.'

'Before you go, there is another matter. I have a customer, named Crispus, who had requested a particularly expensive sculpture to be made for the garden at the entrance to his house. We need to reimburse the artisan for his work and recover our expenses. But the customer has ignored our request for payment for the work carried out on his behalf.'

'It is rumoured that he is selling his wife's expensive jewellery and clothing to pay for his extravagant dinner parties with exotic foods and expensive wines. Perhaps he has a financial problem. I understand that when his wife finds her jewellery or clothing has disappeared, she beats her servants as a punishment.'

He paused before commenting. 'You should check the facts. I expect part of these stories have been reported by the servants, and may not be true. Go and see Petrus sometime today, and he will give you some correct advice on how to handle the matter. Petrus is a property man who understands contract law – a rather pleasant young man.

'Tell Petrus nothing more than the facts – such as the work that was carried out and the delay in payment for the work. Do not report on anything that the servants have said, because it may be simply gossip.'

Julia was disappointed that her father who gives advice in the senate, cannot find time to give his own daughter legal advice. It's like the old tale of the lamplighter who leaves home each evening but ignores the lamps that need oil in his own house.

On second thoughts – perhaps her father will give advice when it becomes crucial.

How can Petrus be of help, she wonders. Perhaps her father envisions him as a potential husband for her, and his daughter becoming remarried following the death of her husband, and secure with a new husband.

The senator, upon departing from Julia, tells his men carrying the litter – to make haste. He has promised to pick up the consul on the way to the senate. It is not one of those occasions where one can arrive late.

The senator reflected upon Julia's appointment with the emperor. He found it difficult to respect an emperor, such as Elagabalus, who cares little about the empire and Rome's historic past.

Later, after leaving the senate, he spoke with his friend, the consul, about young Elagabalus' grandmother Maesa. 'She came to Rome in her position of power soon after the soldiers in Syria declared Elagabalus an emperor. He arrived in

Rome, to join his grandmother, a year later. Upon being in Rome she became known as Julia Maesa.'

The consul said, 'I remember the grandmother arranging for the portrait of her grandson, to be placed in the senate, high above that of the Roman god Jupiter and seeming to disregard the importance of the statue of Victory Nike of Tarentum placed close by.

'It had always been the custom for senators arriving at the senate, to burn an offering to Jupiter and make a libation of wine. The new emperor and an image of his god, Elagabaal, have now been positioned above that of *Jupiter*.

'The statue of the *Victory Nike* of Tarentum with her wings outstretched and standing on a globe, represents peace and victory. The Romans, during the time of the Republic, were involved in war with parts of southern Italy and Sicily, that were being supported by Hannibal.

'I think we have reached a stage where the legions and Praetorian guards nowadays have far more power than the senate – by taking it upon themselves to assassinate and appoint emperors.

'The worry with new emperors, they promise not to kill senators or send them into exile, but they often do – and then provide an obtuse explanation after the killing. Believing that it is too late to argue on the issue and then an emperor collects most of the deceased's assets for his own, personal, imperial account.

'Senators, upon learning about young Elagabalus becoming emperor, when he was appointed in Syria, could not object too much about the appointment as he had the backing of the legions and their belief that Elagabalus was a rightful heir. But these same legions were influenced by the financial offering made to them by the grandmother.'

The senator begins to reminisce. 'I remember when I was a scholar, being told about the ancient wars in Italy – of Hannibal crossing the Alps with his elephants, and making his way to southern Italy, offering to join the fight against the Romans and prevent their plan to incorporate southern Italy within the Roman Republic.

'In those earlier times, Tarentum in the south of Italy, was occupied mainly by Greeks, who were descendants of Sparta, dwelling in the dockside town. It was said that the founders were sons of Spartan woman who had moved to Tarentum.

'They named the port, supposedly after the son of the ancient god *Poseidon*, being *Taras*.

According to the story, *Taras* was shipwrecked and his father sent a dolphin to rescue him. The harbour was named after the Greek nymph *Satyrion* who gave birth to *Taras*.'

'It was the time of Hannibal's Second Punic War, when the fighting spread from the area of Apulia down to southern Tarentum,' said the consul.

'King Phyrrus of Epirus, his homeland, across the Adriatic Sea, also gave support those in southern Italy.

'But when Hannibal departed, the Roman soldiers eventually took over the town and its port. Many of the Greeks were killed or taken as slaves, their property plundered. King Phyrrus – named among the best of Greek Generals, went to Sicily and then returned to his own country to fight other battles.'

The senator recollects, 'Romans collected many artefacts, treasures and sculptures, from southern Italy and had an unencounterable number of copies made of these beautiful marble sculptures and other artefacts.

'When Augustus became first emperor, he placed the statue of *Victory Nike* of Tarentum in the chamber at the Senate, in honour of Rome's *Victory*.'

'Elagabalus does not deserve to have his portrait above that of the goddess *Victory*. He never fought for the people of Rome nor for Italy, where many good men lost their lives,' said the consul.

'More importantly – it is an insult to place himself and his little-known god, above that of *Jupiter*, known to the Greeks as the god *Zeus*,' said the senator.

'But we must consider the question as to why the senate has so little power.'

'The first emperor, Augustus, subtly placed total power of the Roman empire, in the hands of each future emperor, so that no senators can easily remove an emperor, as had happened with Julius Caesar,' said the consul, who continued with his version of the events.

'Emperor Augustus had allowed for future control by emperors, and by the time of Caracalla there were approximately two-thirds of the legions under the control of an emperor. One-third of the legions being under the control of the senate.

'The senatorial controlled provinces were roughly those existing from the time when Rome was a Republic.

'The ever-expanding empire with provinces stretching from Asia Minor to Britain, and the Danube to North Africa, allowed an emperor to have power not only over legions but also auxiliary soldiers who could be used in the provinces or where needed.

'This gave an emperor greater power, but at the same time he was at the mercy of the legions and the commanders.

'Emperor Septimius Severus' advice to his son Caracalla was to "pay the soldiers" – meaning that he should look after those who fought for the emperor.

'When Macrinus became emperor, which position lasted for one year, he ignored such advice, and suffered defeat when grandmother Maesa offered a bribe to the legions to support her grandson, and fight against Macrinus.'

When the senator and the consul arrive at the senator's dwelling, the senator manages to bring up, again, the subject of Elagabalus.

The young emperor was in his thoughts because he was a little worried about his daughter meeting him to discuss garden designs, and whether the emperor was honourable enough to pay for work to be carried out by his daughter.

He began his conversation to show that the grandmother had told a lie when she said that Elagabalus was the son of Caracalla.

'Elagabalus was rumoured to have been born in March 204 – meaning that he was conceived in 203. However, Caracalla had never shown any interest in women or affairs with women, and he was reluctantly forced at the age of fourteen to marry Plautilla whom he disliked immensely, so it seems a fabrication that he would have had a sexual relationship with his cousin, being Elagabalus' mother Soaemias.

'His father, Septimius Severus, was a Libyan man, but his weakness was that he held in high esteem, a fellow Libyan, Plautianus, whom he promoted to the position of Praetorian Prefect. This close friendship allowed the Prefect to express his own self-importance to such an extent that at times he acted as if he were the emperor, having may statues of himself placed around Rome.

'Both Severus and Plautianus agreed that Caracalla should marry Plautianus' daughter, even though this was against Caracalla's wishes.

'The marriage took place and Caracalla had both his new wife and her father-in-law constantly finding fault with all that he did and making his life a misery.

'The young woman was very controlling, to the extent that if she employed a male tutor or any other male worker near her in the dwelling, then that male would have to be castrated, whether the man in question was married or not.'

The consul added, 'Plautianus even had the audacity to try and accuse Julia Domna, the wife of Septimius Severus, of having affairs, which was incorrect. Julia Domna had an interest in Greek philosophy, and mixed in a circle of philosophers. So, there would have been little chance for Caracalla to have had an affair, when he was closely watched by Plautianus, as was his mother.

'When Geta spoke to his brother Severus' about the complaints and abuses the people had suffered from Plautianus, eventually action was taken and the Pretorian Guard's life came to an end in 205 and Caracalla divorced his wife.'

Both the consul and the senator agreed that Elagabalus could not have been the son of Caracalla and that the grandmother had invented the story.

*

Pomegranate cake decorations

The people at Sextus' house now taken their seats in the dining area.

Serving tables are positioned on either side of the room. Huge creative food displays adorn the tables. Large platters of stuffed peacocks, with their long tail feathers enrich some displays, as well as smaller cooked birds, fruits and vegetables on lower display dishes. Other platters contain various types of meat and game pies. Scattered in empty spaces are cleverly designed fruit displays.

Important guests sit nearest the host, in accordance with tradition. But those sitting much further away from the host, although receiving poorer quality food, are appreciative of being on the guest list.

Honoured guests, such as Lucy, are placed close to Sextus, the host. For a little childish humour, Sextus decides to sit Marcus at the furthest end of the table with Papinus to keep him company. Sextus likes Lucy and hopes that he can do a bit of matchmaking between her and Marcus. Possibly encouraging him to chase after her.

The first course is served with precision by several waiters, all dressed in exotic eastern clothing, possibly hired from an outside catering business. Normally Marcus and Sextus eat simple food and will bring in a baker when necessary to cook bread and pastries.

Marcus and Papinus examine their small pieces of fish that had been placed in front of them. Could it be, Marcus wondered, that his miserable piece of fish, looking so unappetising, came from the Tiber river rather that from the waters in the Tyrrhenian Sea?

The Tiber, which flows passed Rome, is where undesirable people are often thrown after they have been beaten up, and body-parts placed in the sewers. But then he remembers that he is more valuable to his uncle being kept healthy and alive.

Papinus is slightly older than Marcus. They have known each other for many years. Papinus steers the conversation towards a statue that he owns – a copy of *Victory*, which he wishes to sell.

'I have a marble statue as well as one or two busts, one of *Odysseus* and the other of *Poseidon*, that I need to sell for financial reason.'

'I know a retired sea captain, Lycus, living in Capri who, most certainly, will be interested,' replies Marcus. 'But I shall pass on the work to Julia. I will ask her to come with me to look at these, especially the *Victory* one.' They arrange a meeting following afternoon.

'How did the statue come into your possession?'

'I regularly go to the library, and sit in the gardens on a stone bench and quietly read – to find inspiration for a poem or speech.' He pauses and looks rather sad.

'One day, I spoke with a young vibrant woman, named Corinna. She worked in the library and we became friendly. Later, she would join me in the gardens and discuss writers.

'We used to sit in the area where there are statues of Greek gods, mainly relating to the sea, and would talk about the myths.

'You may remember that I was married for a while to Corinna.

'Then Tullio from southern Italy came into her life. He was an artist who never produced any works, but Corinna spent many hours encouraging him. On one occasion, when they were in the Library gardens together, he knocked over the *Victory* statue. She said they she would pay the library back weekly for the damage, and brought the broken statue to the house. It was not the original statue of the *Victory*, but a much smaller copy.

'Of course Tullio had no money but she was infatuated with him. Eventually they both left together in their search for happiness. I have the statue, and the other two busts that are mine. I need to repay the library and then I can move on with my life, because my pleasure of going there for books leaves me feeling guilty for not paying for the statue.'

Marcus and Papinus had been so engrossed in their conversation that they barely notice the dinner entertainers. A magician with sleight of hand, who can make scarves or cards disappear or reappear, jugglers, dancers with swirling dresses, and musicians with tambourines, and jugglers.

The guests are served with small biscuits with the letters of the alphabet. Sextus tells them - 'the first person who can make the longest word is to win a prize.' Of course, those at the end of the table know that they are to be served with biscuits with no vowels. Marcus knows all these old tricks. They all clap for the man sitting closest to Sextus who makes up the longest word among those at the table.

Sextus shouts across the table to Marcus. 'Here is a riddle – see if you can give me the answer. What is the strongest of all things?'

Marcus believes that everyone at the table knows the answer. He was going to be sarcastic, but then decides to act out the scene to add a little humour to the occasion.

He stands in front of the guests. 'Iron is stronger.' He moves his arms as if lifting an imaginary weight. Everyone gives a laugh.

He continues: 'The blacksmith is stronger.' Then acts if he is lifting the world above his head. More laughter. Lowering his voice as if revealing a secret. 'The answer to your question is love – love can subdue a blacksmith.' Marcus then acts out as if he is a man in love, and dances around as if he is under a spell. 'So love is the stronger.' Everyone claps.

Household slaves often feel more superior in knowledge than their masters. Papinus can hear one of them mutter to himself, 'Iron is the stronger – love is an emotion.'

Sextus the matchmaker has produced no spark between Marcus and Lucy. He decides to move things along by touching Lucy's hand, then a little while later her neck, and then touching her shoulder to speak quietly to her.

The next course is served.

Waiters working at the lower end of the table are somewhat over-exaggerating an effeminate walk, and pose when they present their trays of food. Whilst the distraction is taking place, another waiter slips some food into a pocket under his apron.

In accordance with Roman custom, the guests seated further away from the host are provided with coarse pottery and a cheap thick glass and bone cutlery. Whilst Lucy and other honoured guests have silver and gold edged plates, and cutlery of the finest silver trimmed with gold. Their wine glasses are tinted red in colour with gold laurel leaf designs.

Lucy has white bread, soft and easy to fall apart. Marcus' bread is nearly black in colour and its texture is very gritty. As he stretches his arm across the table to retrieve a soft bread roll, a waiter removes it and replaces the good bread with the gritty flour variety.

Marcus laughs when Papinus' remarks that there is even a difference in the colourful peacock feathers pointing upwardly to the host, and the dull ones pointing downwards at the lowly guests. It is as if even the plucked feathers recognise the difference.

Still, the food is plentiful if one takes the trouble to keep asking the waiter to bring more, eventually he returns with better cuts or servings. Guests can also ask, at the end of the meal, for some to be wrapped up so that they can take it home, as is the custom, but not all people take up the offer.

Calling for more drinks, Marcus notices a wine waiter, one of the household servants, partially hidden behind a curtain. He is swigging from a jug of the best wine, and re-filling it with a cheaper wine. He then brings the jug to their table. Marcus asks him to replace it with another, now wondering if the waiter will bring him the best or the poorest quality wine.

Calling across the room in a loud voice, for his uncle to hear: 'What vintage is this wine – is it really from the lower regions?'

'Most definitely from the lower regions – let the waiters provide you with some more.' Sextus replies with humour in his voice, holding one hand near his pelvic area.

'This definitely is a great challenge to the pallet,' responds Marcus.

They both know their wines well, since that is their main source of business.

Marcus decides to walk over to where Lucy and Sextus are seated, to see whether they have better quality cakes to eat. He intends to take some back for Papinus and himself, and can see that there are small cakes with different types of decorations which look appetising.

Lucy has been having trouble with Sextus. He is constantly touching her, gently in a kindly fatherly way, but nonetheless it is annoying. As if she were his pet toy.

'I wonder how they do the embroidery on your robe. My wife used to have clothing with beautiful workmanship.' He touches the embroidery close to her arm.

'It's hard to eat my cake if you hold my arm – could you put your hand down?' She asks in a kindly manner.

Lucy decides to take matters into her own hands.

She carefully takes the sapphire pin from the top of her hair. Discretely she removes the red pill from beneath the blue stone and proceeds to place it on top of a small cake alongside those decorated with pomegranate pips, close to where Sextus is sitting.

Marcus arrives at the table and surprises her, and she tries to retrieve the cake with the red pill.

She is a little slow – Marcus picks up the small dainty cake. Lucy attempts to take it out of his hand.

Like a magic trick, Marcus waives the cake in circles in front of her hand as she tries to grab it away from him.

In a teasing gesture, he moves the cake back and forth to her, and as she tries to reach it to take it from him – he quickly pops the small cake into his mouth.

Lucy is speechless.

CHAPTER TWO

Dreams, Illusions and Reality of Emperors

It is dusk when Julia arrives at Sextus' house. She is tired after visiting the emperor, with no time left to meet up with Petrus to discuss Crispus, and his non-payment of the bill for the statue in his garden.

Approaching the dining area, she can see Lucy stooping down on the opposite side of the table, she is supporting Marcus' head as his body lies slumped on the floor.

Julia hurries over.

Lucy explains the whole situation about the poisoning, and Marcus swallowing the red pill intended for Sextus.

Marcus can hear what she is saying, but does not have the strength to move his head in their direction.

The two women explain to Sextus that it must have been something Marcus had eaten. At their fabricated story, he now understands that he is in a fantasy world of fibs, and that Lucy had popped a red pill on the cake.

He wants to raise his eyebrows in amazement at the story they are giving to Sextus, but his eyebrows seem to collaborate with the women by refusing to rise upward to show amazement.

Marcus is taken to a bedroom. Sextus' doctor, who examines Marcus to diagnose the problem, returns to Sextus' study to report on his findings, saying that Marcus will be all right in a couple of hours. Perhaps it was something he had eaten.

Sextus has all the cooks beaten for poisoning the food. They said the food was carefully prepared, but their pleas are ignored.

The doctor is more concerned about the health of the older man than Marcus. Sextus informs the doctor that he is fine. Adding. 'Next time I go for an examination, perhaps the "good doctor" will not bring in cold-fingered trainees to prod my body, otherwise I may die of frostbite before my time!'

The doctor does not reveal his opinion, that Marcus had probably been given a drug or sedative. He had seen a number of strange cases of late.

It was only a few weeks back when emperor Elagabalus had asked him to make an opening in his lower abdomen so that he could have a woman's vagina as well as keeping his circumcised penis. The circumcision was carried out in accordance with his Syrian religious beliefs. The doctor's training had taught him to never show surprise. He refused to meet with the young emperor's request to provide him with a vagina. He had heard the rumours that Elagabalus liked to go to brothels and act out the role of a prostitute.

Julia tells Lucy to go home, and that she will stay until Marcus recovers. Julia knows that she will not be able to sleep worrying about Marcus' health, and thinking how her father will be furious if he learns that Marcus has been poisoned by Lucy.

She asks Lucy to visit Petrus in the morning and explain to him about Crispus and to ask for advice on what they should do to recoup the money.

Julia has already decided upon a plan to arrange a show room event for customers to view the latest products. Her intention is to invite Messalina, a close dining companion of Crispus, hoping that Messalina will leak out news to her on Crispus' financial position.

Now, unable to make that visit to speak with Petrus, she needs Lucy to see Messalina on her behalf.

Julia tells Lucy to mention to Messalina, when she visits her, that only exclusive customers will be invited to the showroom, as well as a few prominent men.

'If you are pushed to give one of the names, then mention Sextus, but otherwise just say that you do not remember.'

Messalina always likes to have invitations and make notes in her diary of daily events. She prefers people who will treat her to meals or holidays, and in return they may be gifted, or re-gifted, with an old item she does not want any more, but she makes the receiver imagine that they are receiving a gift that is precious.

A long time ago, she was married to an aristocrat, whose name she would mention regularly, but barely has any contact with him or his family after he re-married. Everyone in turn, after hearing snippets of her news, would then name-drop to show that they were in the inner circle of second-hand news about an aristocrat.

'Prominent men' to Messalina is like offering a parrot its favourite nut. She likes to consider herself as still being in the inner circle. Any man of prominence must be contacted and coerced into making contact with her.

She has a daily routine, to keep closely connected with all her friends to find out if any one of them knows a man of prominence. A letter, and even a gift, is then sent by her to the man and a further follow up takes place just in case he has not made immediate contact. The newcomer eventually becoming a new entry name in her diary.

'Leave it to me,' replies Lucy, when parting from Julia with all the necessary instructions.

Ndio says that she will stay with Julia at Sextus' house.

Julia says to Sextus, 'I will stay at your house, to take care of Marcus until he recovers - my maid shall also stay. Hopefully his recovery is quick and he is out of your house by morning.'

Sextus had a little chuckle at the thought of Marcus being turfed out of the house by Julia.

Returning to the bedroom, she sees that Marcus appears very hot, and his face perspiring. Julia sits on the side of the bed and wipes his face with cool water. He is still in a deep sleep.

Eventually, Ndio can see that both Marcus and Julia are asleep and does not wish to disturb them. She settles for the night on the carpeted floor nearest the door, and collects a cushion for her head and a blanket from the back of a chair.

Before closing her eyes, Ndio gazes at the moonlight coming through the open window. Beams of light and shade fall across the wall. Then she notices a painting on the wall of the bedroom - it is a portrait of a young man who looks exactly like Marcus, but without a beard and shorter hair.

Soon all three were asleep.

*

Dreams – resembling reality.

Gundher sits on a chair in his bedroom feeling too tired to sleep. He thinks about his visit to the palace earlier in the day with Julia who, prior to the meeting, agreed to meet him in the courtyard of the palace grounds.

He has been a freedman for several years, and is now looking after Julia's business interests by liaising with the artisans, buildings, workmen, and most of all the sculptors that had their own guilds or colleges. Like his father, he has worked for Julia's father, Quintus, all his life.

Upon meeting Julia, he immediately slapped muddy water from a nearby puddle, across the lower part of her leg.

'Why did you do that? I've just smartened myself up for this business meeting!'

Gundher noticed her surprise when he spoke. 'Well Elagabalus doesn't like to have affairs with women who have a slight imperfection. So please explain it away as a scar.'

'I'm not planning to marry him. It's a business meeting, I don't intend to become the emperor's wife. Now remove that mess.'

'No, your father told me to protect you.' Gundher still had an obligation towards her father, the patriarch of the family.

As she walked through the courtyard, a small white dog came up to her leg and started sniffing it.

He smiles when he remembers how she turned around to him saying, 'I hope this dog did not pee in the muddy water which you placed on my leg!'

She then gave him a friendly grin as she is taken, by a palace escort, to meet Elagabalus.

Gundher remained near the palace gates, waiting to be called. He began a conversation with a guard near the gate.

'What is it like to follow Elagabalus around and not be visiting the provinces and seeing places around the empire? It seems that the young emperor likes to remain static.'

The guard replied. 'The young emperor is not of the same calibre as emperor Septimius Severus.'

'My father served with Septimius Severus when, in 193, the legions came down from the Danube to Rome. The reason being, to avenge the deaths of two earlier emperors. Commodus who was assassinated at the end of 192, which brought into effect the immediate appointment of the emperor Pertinax in January 193, who was also assassinated in March of the same year, with nobody being held responsible.

'Severus had spoken with legion commanders based on the Danube borders, for them to choose their best men to march with him to Rome to find those responsible, as the duty of palace guards is to protect emperors.

'Six hundred strong men chosen from various legions on the Danube, set off from Carnumtum, around 683 miles northeast of Rome.

'Their mission, for the chosen men, was to make their way to Rome as quickly as possible to prevent the present emperor, Julianus, from organizing his legions, navy or the Praetorian Guard from attacking them.

'They moved silently overland, not drawing attention to themselves, and not knowing whether the local people were supporters of Julianus, the present emperor, or supporters of Septimius Severus who was marching with the men towards Rome.

'With a need to stay vigilant they wore full battle gear, including breastplates, and carried basic food supplies, a cloak for warmth and some basic cooking equipment for the whole of their journey. Covering the distance possibly took around three weeks or more, travelling around 30 miles a day with full pack and having to set up camp and cook their food each night.

'Severus stayed alongside his men day and night, resting only when absolutely necessary. He slept with them in makeshift tents, suffering the same hardships and shared the same food, just as soldiers had done at the time of Trajan.

'The men respected Severus, because as a leader he had the ability to take on complex situations. He sent messages to various commanders under the control of the emperor Julianus, requesting them to switch support, and avoid unnecessary fighting. He requested weapons to be placed at various points, and for the navy based at Ravenna on the northwest coast of Italy to switch sides.'

'I remember hearing stories,' said Gundher, 'that, following the deaths of Commodus and Pertinax in Rome, Julianus was only elected emperor by auction held by the soldiers in Rome. Julianus had offered them a better financial deal.

'Pertinax, the previous emperor prior to the auction appointment of Julianus, was assassinated when some two to three hundred *equites singulars,* part of the personal guard, marched fully armed and in wedge formation, from their camp to the imperial residence. Their dissatisfaction was due to financial cut-backs which Pertinax felt he was forced to make as he predecessor Commodus had recklessly caused financial problems.

'Guards on duty at the palace would have heard the noise of angry marching men – yet they made no attempt to protect the palace and, most of all, failed to carry out their duty to protect the emperor.

'Outnumbered, somewhat foolhardy, yet unafraid, Pertinax made his way to hear their complaints. He tried to offer them assurances. Some showed respect but, unexpectedly, one of the men leaped forward and thrust out his sword, and the others joined in with the cowardly attack.

'They cut off Pertinax' head and placed it on a spear.'

Gundher paused, whilst both men were momentarily lost in thought, 'I heard that the senate was surrounded, when the guards made their decision, and senators feared for their lives because some had been supporters of Pertinax, and some had been involved earlier with Julianus when finding him guilty of various offences. The people did not fully approve of the appointment of Julianus.'

The guard commented, 'With the support of commanders of fifteen legions on the Danube, Septimius Severus also was given support by the governor of Britain, Clodius Albinus, who also held sway with several legions under his command.

'It was said that back in Rome, Julianus upon learning that Septimius Severus was making his way south towards Rome, that the emperor gave orders for men to train with elephants, which were generally used for ceremonial purposes, but now had to convert to warfare. The elephants objected to the towers placed on their backs and would throw the men and equipment onto the ground. Orders to construct ramparts and ditches were given to the guards, who had become unaccustomed to physical labour.

'The march into Rome by Septimius and his men was without bloodshed. Upon entering Rome they were welcomed by the senate who already had passed a death sentence on Didius Julianus.'

'I enjoyed hearing about your father. You must be very proud of him,' said Gundher.

Before they could continue their conversation further, Gundher was called to join Julia with the emperor Elagabalus to find out what sort of work he required for the fountain.

Elagabalus was dressed in his priestly robes with glittery stones twinkling as he moved his body. He wore numerous necklaces, eye makeup and his lips were painted red.

'I am rather tired, so I can't give you a lot of time. But I can tell you what I require and then you can go and prepare some nice drawings in order that I can make a decision.'

He had overslept and would have liked to remain in bed. The previous evening, he set aside a room at the palace to entertain his close friends. They knew the theme of the party.

His workers had earlier put up a gold-ringed curtain at the doorway entrance at the entertainment room at the palace.

The evening began with him greeting friends in a sultry, sensual voice. Each person entered through the ringed curtains where they had to present Elagabalus with a coin. On the observe side was the outline of winglets of the Roman god Mercury and the rod and two snakes twirling together. On the reverse side was a sexual depiction. Such coins were often produced in taverns for entrance to the inner rooms.

Courtesans, male and female, liked to receive palace invitations. They dressed for the evening in see-through garments of silk. Or silk clothes in bright yellow colours. Many of

Elagabalus' male friends would remove all their public hair and wear cosmetics and paint their nails and wear cosmetics.

But after a long night of indulgence, and a long morning bathing with his friends in scented water and flower petals, he presented lethargic and tired appearance, when meeting Julia to discuss the pond feature.

Upon being asked about his ideas for a garden feature, Elagabalus had finally decided upon a fountain that spurted water down into an elongated pond, and requested one or two statues positioned around the edges.

Julia suggested some designs, such an oval shaped pond, and painting the inside black so that the sun or moonlight was easily reflected upon the water. She felt that he may like a statue of the god *Narcissus*, leaning at the water's edge. The emperor quite liked that idea.

He remarked, 'One of the pleasures will be looking up at the sky and the sun – then glancing into the pond and viewing reflections of sunlight in the water.' He began musing about his sun god, Elagabaal. 'In the evenings on a moonlit night I will be able to watch the reflection of the moon on the clear water and myself wearing my priestly robes. The more I think about it, the more I like the idea of a statue of *Narcissus.*'

'Where do you intend to place this fountain and pond?' asked Gundher.

'Contact me when you have prepared your drawings and we will discuss this further,' he replied.

Gundher, sitting in his bedroom at the end of a long day, reflected a little upon the conversation he had with the guard, who had mentioned emperor Commodus, the son of Marcus Aurelius. Marcus Aurelius was known for his Stoic philosophy and a good emperor, but unfortunately the son did not follow for long in his father's footsteps because his behaviour became erratic. After Commodus' death the senate quickly elected Pertinax as emperor.

During Commodus' erratic years, it caused senators to be concerned for their own lives.

Rumours went around that the emperor wished to align himself with the god *Hercules*, and his clothing was to change from the less ornate Roman style, which emperors had copied over the years, to donning a lion skin cloak and clasping a club.

It was widely known that he appeared in the amphitheatre, on one occasion, attempting to re-enact one of the mythical labours of *Hercules*.

According to ancient myth, the demi-god had to kill a great flock of crane size, man-eating *Stymphalian* birds ... a task carried out by using a stone, sling and bow.

It seems that Commodus performed his version of the task when he entered a full amphitheatre clothed as *Hercules* – but there were no *Stymphalian* birds – his shots were at the spectators.

Gundher had heard gossip that many senators were not too upset at the assassination of Commodus, as there were periods when they feared for their own lives.

He decides that it is time, to go to bed. Neatly folding his clothes, he went to his bed naked.

*

One person who manages to sleep easily is Sextus. He is curled up in bed surrounded by his large, duck-feathered pillows dreaming that he has his arms around his wife. She had died long ago but the memories and dreams of her companionship are still with him. He has aged physically, but in his mind and dreams he is still a young forty-year old. Any dreams he has of himself are always as a youngish man. When not asleep, he mentally believes himself to be that age. His brain overcoming the physical body.

Aging he felt was for the onlooker. Only when looking into a mirror does he come face to face with an image he does not recognise - an older self. Who is that stranger? A trick of mind, or eye? Was it *Zeus'* hoodwink?

Everyone is in a dream world in the Sextus household.

*

A threesome thwarts serenity

Papinus at his farm was attempting to read before sleep, but his thoughts keep returning to the time when he first met Corinna, the love of his life.

Whilst searching for a particular book made of the finest vellum, in Rome's public library. he met Corinna. In amongst the collection of scrolls of the literary works on shelves and in the honeycombed book display sections, she would find him particular writings by ancient poets, whose busts were exhibited in niches built into sections of the walls.

From the time they first met, he knew that there was a spark. During her lunch breaks they would sit together in the library grounds and peruse some of the works.

Papinus would sit on a stone bench beneath a tree for shade, free from the bright sunlight. Low walls divided the sections around the gardens where statues or busts of famous Romans or Greeks were on display. His favourite spot was where the statues of the ancient gods and goddesses such as *Artemis, Aphrodite, Poseidon* and *Athena* and *Ares* were situated.

He took inspiration for his plays or poems from the writers of Greek tragedies, such as *Aeschylus,* who produced a play about '*Agamemnon*' who was a main character in Homer's Trojan War, *The Iliad. Sophocles* wrote the tragedy of '*Electra*', who was the daughter of *Agamemnon*. Tragedies were for the thinking man, and favourites of the senators, who preferred these plays rather than attending the amphitheatre where killing of animals and prisoners were held.

On occasions Corinna and Papinus would sit close to a Roman copy of the statue of

Nike/Athena. A fine marble statue of the goddess, *Athena,* or *Victory* sculptured as if standing on the prow of a ship. Wind seemed to blow against her soft, flowing clothing.

The fine workmanship of the carver took the viewer into a world of imagination – the carver of the marble creates the softness of touch for the skin. Very thin layers of marble provide the impression that it is thin clothing covering part of her body. Her wings opening out as if to catch the wind, and her body is turned to produce a counter-balance as if to move with the ship and the waves of the sea.

The library carvings were not the original size – but smaller copies made by Greeks living in southern Italy, using the same translucent, white marble from Paros, an island halfway between Athens and Rhodes. The ships' base being of a darker and non-translucent stone. It was carved in respect of the goddess to commemorate a very ancient Greek sea battle. Mariners believed that she had protected their lives and helped them achieve a victory.

It was in this tranquil setting that Papinus asked Corinna to marry him, and believed that she was his muse. She inspired his creative writing.

She moved to his middle-sized farm, which had a smallish traditional farmhouse and a barn. Further away were the farm workers living quarters. These families had been with his family for generations.

When writing in his study, she would act out the roles of certain historical stories so that he could recreate his version of the tales to his present-day readers or listeners.

Spreading herself across a pile of cushions against the back of a sofa, she pretended it one of the Sabine women being spirited away by a man on a horse and taken to Rome. As happened to the women in the story when the Sabine women were kidnapped, which had been written over two hundred years earlier by the Roman historian *Livy*. But Papinus was using his own version of this ancient event.

When the founders of Rome were in need of women to help them have wives and offspring and build their city they resorted to kidnapping women from a nearby Italian area.

Papinus, whilst Corinna was bouncing around up and down on the back of the sofa, decided to take his story back a little further to the time of the end Trojan War, when Aeneas, whose mother was

Aphrodite (*Venus*), was able to leave Troy with his father, and make his way to Carthage where he was attracted to Queen Dido, and she fell madly in love with him. But spiritually he was aware that he must leave and make his way to Italy, and help with the founding of a city. He first went to Sicily and the western Italy, when the history of Rome began.

Other roles that Corinna liked to act out included a scene about *Perseus* rescuing *Andromeda*, which she hoped would inspire Papinus.

His muse would act out the mythical role of being *Andromeda*, chained naked to a rock. The local town's people had chained *Andromeda*, in the mythical story, to appease a sea serpent or sea-dragon. The monster had been resting by their water supply, and they thought this offering was the best way to obtain their water and satisfy the creature.

Corinna played the role of *Andromeda*. She loosely tied herself to the first post, or newel post, of the staircase, pretending that it was the rock to which *Andromeda* had been chained. Corinna imagined the water rising around her and any time soon the sea monster would make a grab at her.

The more the imagined water rose, the more she panted. Her breasts and tied hands were moving up and down, breathing, screaming, panting and yelling. She liked to overact her parts.

It did cause Felix, his headman, picking fruit off the trees close to the house, at the time of Corinna panting and screaming, to look through the window. He thought that she was being murdered.

Instead, Papinus was sitting at his desk writing furiously. It did not look as if Corinna wanted to be rescued – at least not by a servant. Perhaps it was more of an earthy orgasmic sound than screams of help. Felix never knew the story of *Andromeda*, nor about the sea serpent-dragon and the coming of *Perseus*.

He assumed that she desperately wanted sex and Papinus had to keep her lustful behaviour on the other side of the room whilst he quietly wrote. How could he do that, he wondered when she was heaving and writhing for sex.

He told all the other slaves what he saw, and they gave their version of the event. It livened up their evenings whilst they sat outdoors by their fire.

Felix enjoyed reporting all this gossip back to Papinus who thought it very amusing.

Papinus created many illusionary stories relating to the myths and was paid small amounts of money for his written works.

Now that he was slightly wealthier, Corinna wanted a larger house. Papinus said that it would be built next to their present one. He had no intention of moving away from the farm. She enjoyed decorating the new house and buying furniture, and keeping all the older items in the older cottage.

Soon their lives changed.

Tullio, an artist, came into their lives.

He also met Corinna at the library and began painting her portrait at the end of each afternoon in the grounds where she had previously met Papinus. His work was so slow and he never quite finished each drawing, nor got around to putting paint on any of his efforts.

Corinna began to return late back from work. She said that she was trying to encourage Tullio to become successful, and that Papinus must be patient.

One day Tullio accidentally knocked over the sculpture of the *Victory*. The library wanted him to pay for a replacement, but he had no money nor possessions.

Corinna agreed to repay the money for the breakage, a little each week from her earnings, and brought the damaged statue back to the barn. She also brought Tullio to the house because the library no longer wanted him on their premises.

She helped to make a studio for him in the smaller house, regardless of Papinus' protests, and he was coerced into buying the sponger an easel and painting material.

'It was only to be a temporary arrangement until he sells his paintings and repays damages,' said Corinna.

Papinus wanted to know more about this man who had come into their lives – this interloper.

'Where do you come from? What is the name of your family?' Papinus asks Tullio.

Tullio replies, 'I can't answer questions because it is stopping my artistic and philosophical thought.'

What philosophical artistic thought? Papinus considered that his own fruit picker had more power of reasoning than Tullio.

Papinus considers it strange that 'artistic thought' was not stronger than his emotional desire for another man's wife. There was no proof that he was ever an artist – he is just a trickster who easily manipulates Corinna into giving him free accommodation and money.

Papinus as a writer, whose works involve story creation and make-believe, now he feels his real world is being encapsulated by Tullio's manipulation and possessive desires.

Initially it was just simple requests, when making himself more settled and comfortable in Papinus' cottage, then came requests for paints and easels, but lately he fenced off a patch of garden in which to sunbathe.

Papinus grew to dislike the con artist.

'Please leave him alone – I don't think you understand, Tullio is an imaginative thinker and painter.

'You just don't understand,' said Corinna repeating herself, 'Tullio believes in simple happiness and pleasure and freedom from mental anxiety,' she said in his defence.

Turning to Corinna he said, 'I believe Tullio could not be following the philosophical thinking of Diogenes, who was content to live in a ceramic jar. So why doesn't Tullio follow the example set by Diogenes. Perhaps I should go out and find him a large jar!'

'Or perhaps he is a follower of Epicureanism – a life of tranquillity and pleasure.

'His ideal of happiness only works if he sponges off others. Ridding himself of mental anxiety, by not paying for his keep. Perhaps it is time for him think of others - and their happiness. He could take an interest in a spot of work, such as helping on the farm – otherwise must find outside work and pay off the library and become a responsible man.'

Papinus did regret his comments, but he was reaching the end of his tether, with this intruder wanted everything that Papinus has, and until recently enjoyed. It is very unusual for him to lose his temper. He is normally such a quiet man.

Corinna went off to bed in a huff.

He remembers how sad he was when he went to sleep on his large sofa by the fire with his dogs next to him. He did not wake up until late the next morning.

In the kitchen he found a note from Corinna saying: 'Tullio and I have seized the moment of truth. We are passionate about each other. We are off to find love and nature.'

Although they were in their romantic illusion of wonderland, Papinus on the other hand was left to find the money to repay the library for their loss – there was still a large sum outstanding.

Several months had gone by since those miserable days, but now he is hopeful that Marcus will to be able to sell the statue and this can provide him with money to clear off his debt.

He enjoyed the evening at Sextus' house and the company of Marcus. But he left Sextus' dinner party soon after Marcus went over to where Lucy and Sextus were sitting.

His book remained unopened. He was completely exhausted, his dogs nudged his hand to let him know that they were there, and he went into a peaceful sleep.

*

The senator could not sleep. He thought about Elagabalus.

He picked up a scroll from his bed stand and began to read about the days of Cato the Younger – one of the men who brought about Julius Caesar's reason to cross the Rubicon and enter Rome. A civil war ensued which led to Julius Caesar becoming emperor.

Julius Caesar wanted to rule in perpetuity, which caused the senators to have him killed.

The Roman Republic ceased to exist not long after the death of Julius Caesar. The senator's thoughts then went to the Roman Empire, and the first emperor being Augustus, Julius Caesar's named heir. Many emperors have followed on until the present time, which is two hundred and twenty years later.

The senator dropped off to sleep, and later a servant came into his bedroom and turned out the lamp. He neatly placed the scroll of Cato the Younger next to the one of Cato the Elder. Both were the senator's favourite reading material.

*

Marcus had been having nightmares, being chased by wild animals. He awakes from his drugged sleep and looks through slit eyes.

Close to his head is a creature with large circular black eyes and black hair covering its head and neck. Upon opening his eyes wider, he realises that it is Julia – her black mascara had run around her eyes and had intermingled with her tears when she was worried about Marcus – and her hair extensions were in a horrid mess.

Making an effort to sit up, he realises Julia's arm is across his chest. He knows she will not wish to be caught, looking like she had escaped from an animal fight in the arena, so he closed his eyes again – allowing her a bit of dignity, but with a smile on his face holding back his laughter.

He realises that his nightmares were probably caused worries about the business. In a few months' time shipping is halted during the winter months, but in the meantime he needs to sell what is in their storage as well as obtain orders for the following year. Besides wines he also buys and sells good quality raisins that have been dried in the sun and imported or exported in a packaged condition.

Whilst travelling around and visiting ports and vineyards, he became aware of the problems when ships are held up in ports, bad weather at sea, and sometimes theft from warehouses. Time is wasted sorting out customs duty and documentation at the docks in various countries which all have different provincial procedures that holds back progress. It was good to learn about the business whilst undercover, but he hopes Sextus will not fully retire because they work well together.

He had been in a deep sleep and needed to get back to work.

Julia is still in slumber so he gently eases himself out of the bed and goes to find clothes and bathe. Ndio had left the room much earlier.

CHAPTER THREE

Taking Care of Statues and Figurines

Earlier in the morning sunlight was shining in the bedroom where Marcus had been placed for the night after being drugged. Ndio, awoke and looks again at the portrait on the wall and can clearly see the remarkable resemblance to Marcus, except the man in the painting does not wear a beard. She realises that he is related to Sextus, as both men had treated each other with easy familiarity, especially when they were gathered around the pond the previous day.

She decides not to mention it to Julia until she has more facts.

Julia upon awakening, finds a note from Marcus saying that they must meet at Papinus' farm, early afternoon and briefly mentions the statues which Papinus wishes to sell, and informs her that he has a prospective buyer. She will be able to make some money on the deal.

Finishing off his note he adds: 'Thank your staff for their attempts to kill me last night – good thing that I have a sense of humour.

*

A dragon's surprise

The street address Julia gave to Lucy only provides her with brief information as to the whereabouts of Messalina's apartment. But in reality, she sees many apartments in the area all looking very similar.

The only map she knows is the Severus Marble Plan and Forma Urbis Romae marble slabs, which measures 18 x 10 metres. She wonders how she can reduce the plan all to fit onto her small wax tablet, which she holds in her hand. Eighteen metres she remembers as being eighteen paces. Her mind is fixed on her tablet whilst she tries to work out mathematical reductions.

Fortunately, a man, after watching Lucy pace up and down several times, and frequently looking at her wax tablet – offers his assistance. She tells him her problem. He knows where the building is, and he walks with her up to the front of the premises.

Approaching the *insula*, or apartment block, there are some shops on the ground floor. Looking up at the building she notices that the first floor has balconies, other floors are without, whilst the top two floors seem to be constructed of wood, with no fancy frontage.

Messalina's apartment is on the first floor and Lucy makes her way up the stairs and along the corridor.

She can see that Messalina has left her door open. But upon reaching the doorway, facing an approaching visitor is a metal figure of a wolf or dragon's head, with its mouth open, showing fierce teeth and long red tongue. The head is mounted on a long horizontal pole and attached to the wall, at head-height. Flowing from the head is the body. An elongated red strip of fabric with tiny crocodile leg appendages – supposedly dragon or stick thin wolf legs.

Julia had warned her that the host likes to play games and be impish. Lucy does not feel in the mood – she just needs to rest after poisoning

Marcus the previous evening, and she has barely slept with worry.

The entrance door is ajar, and the passageway causes a breeze, which makes the fabric to balloon out and sway around as if the dragon-wolf is ready to attack.

Lucy finds a moment when the wind does not blow, and the Draco's head not facing towards her – then she knocks.

A voice comes from within the apartment. 'Come in – I hope my Dacian Draco didn't frighten you. Don't forget to take your shoes off.'

As she stands on the mat to take off her shoes she notices, as she is standing on a doormat. Painted on the mat is a circular shaped head with big eyes, and hair looking like masses of snakes with eyes, and give the impression of looking up her dress. She guessed that it was another of Messalina's fun way to greeting visitors.

She thought that she must remember the doormat when she leaves the apartment.

Through a short hallway she enters the main apartment living room.

Lucy notices a sixty-year old woman doing a handstand against the opposite wall. Her skimpy strip or band of material covering her breasts, and small fitting material covering a tiny portion of her lower body, allowed a great flow of excess skin with no support. Her skin had ceased to grow in the right places. Or had overgrown in the wrong places and it seems definitely misplaced when seen upside down.

'Oh, I was expecting Julia.'

'Don't you think I have nice legs?' Forcing Lucy to take a very quick glance.

'I used to ride horses, and do a spot of chariot racing years ago, on my father's land,' she pauses for a compliment.

Lucy just murmurs.

She looks around the room, to avoid any further gaze at Messalina in her minute bikini underwear. Then fixes her attention on some small Greek ornamental bowls, depicting ancient Greek dancing figures.

Lucy has mostly seen these figures painted on the inside of the bowls, but these bowls are covered with pomegranate pips, or dried lavender heads. Probably not what the potter's artist intended.

The hostess likes to embarrass people or challenge them when being ignored. She then quickly reverts to childlike fussing and tittering, by demanding attention to cause a stir.

Messalina stands up, and moves closer to Lucy. Loudly she says, 'I hope I didn't embarrass you - let me go put on some clothes.'

Annoyingly to Lucy, she continued: 'Are you blushing – are you embarrassed? Oh, I must tell Julia that you are shy and embarrassed.'

Lucy felt nothing of the sort – just annoyance, with this woman and her nonsense.

'I hope I didn't surprise you by standing on my head. I do it every morning. Something I learned at India many years ago. I had met a wonderful man who was writing about his religious beliefs. He told me that it was a good thing for me to do – standing on my head, that is!'

Messalina wanted to impress Lucy by making it seem that she only knew intelligent people. 'I think he was a sage or wise man.'

'Oh,' said Lucy, trying not to be supercilious or smug. 'You, as a young lady, and being asked by a man to do handstands in your undergarments, I am sure he was a special mentor to you!'

Messalina continues. 'He would sit on his terrace watching me in the mornings or late afternoon practice handstands up against the wall

– a few times I fell and he would catch me and help me up again.'

'You were lucky to have such a mentor – and I am sure he was a man of many convincing charms and techniques.'

Deep down, Lucy thought that it took place many years ago, when Messalina was many years younger with her intelligent visionary or so-called mentor! But she had the nagging question as to whether Messalina was naïve or controlling the man to suit her own needs.

Having little reaction from Lucy, eventually Messalina left to put on some clothes.

'So why couldn't Julia come?' She startles Lucy who is enjoying her few moments of peace. Now, she is caught off-guard – not expecting to be questioned on Julia's absence.

'Julia had to attend an unexpected meeting with Papinus.'

'Was there a reason why she had to see him urgently?' Messalina was playing a game of being the hunter with a deer.

Lucy mumbles, 'I think it could be something to do with herbs for the showroom.' Looking at the seeds in the pots quickly brought the idea of plants to mind.

'What sort of herbs?' Messalina is beginning to feel jealous that Papinus is getting Julia's attention and she felt more important than Papinus whom she barely knows.

'I think it was lavender,' Lucy lies.

Mention the name of someone who is in the limelight, and the next thing for Messalina is that Papinus' name must be added to her address book and make him become her close friend.

What Lucy had told Messalina was like a red flag to a charging goat - something to devour.

She decides to find a reason to contact him. Perhaps write a personal letter to get to know Papinus a little better, or to catch him in the street so that she can to tell him about herself.

It was like stealing another child's toy. To have him as her own personal friend – closer to her than with Julia. But Messalina needed to act fast if she is to interfere in the friendship between Julia and Papinus.

She needs more facts. 'Why would Julia want lavender?'

'I don't know. We never discussed it. Perhaps it was for tiny displays on presents with a few ribbons attached for the showroom event – or simply just to give to the guests.'

Lucy decides that it is time to leave.

'Your Dacian dragon did give me a surprise – I'm not quite sure if it has the head of a dragon or a wolf. It's quite frightening when it's flying horizontally – makes one feel as if it's ready to bite.'

Lucy was pleased to exit the apartment – but first she has to put on her shoes yet not wish to stand on the spot of the doormat, where a painted *Gorgon*'s head with snake hair, and large eyes peers upwards. She recalls that the ancient writer Homer had mentioned *Agamemnon,* who fought against the Trojans, having the depiction of a *Gorgon* on his shield. She felt like one of *Agamemnon*'s enemies – except scared by not the shield, but the doormat.

Walking in the street was pleasant – away from all the questioning.

In her school days she had to study Trajan's column in Rome. The column depicts the emperor's first battle that took place with the Getae-Dacians a hundred years earlier.

Trajan made a second attempt to crush the Dacian king, Decebalus, whose territory covered Romania, Transylvania and Serbia, close to the Danube River. Trajan won this battle, which gave access to Rome, or perhaps it was the emperor, to acquired several gold and silver mines and trading access down to the Mediterranean or the Adriatic coast.

Before he died, Decebalus took refuge in the Carpathian Mountains. Upon being cornered, he slit his own throat. He knew he would have been paraded through the streets of Rome, and then killed in an undignified manner.

Romans soldiers, upon discovering his body, cut off his head and hands. These eventually reached Rome and were thrown down the Gemonian flight of steps near the Mamertine prison, close by the Forum, where prisoners await execution.

Prisoners, who were unfortunate to be held in the prison in Rome, waiting to die, were tied up, strangled, and thrown onto the steps for the public and animals and birds to abuse the bodies.

The final ending for all these prisoners, including the remains of Decebalus, went into the Tiber River or in smaller pieces into the sewer system.

Lucy remembers learning at school that the Romans admitted to the fact that Decebalus was a great 'barbarian' warrior. Anyone who did not share Roman customs, was considered a barbarian, regardless of their own ancient cultures or kingly rule.

After the death of Decebalus, Dacia became part of the Roman Empire, and a cohort of Dacian military auxiliaries was formed. It became common practice to use auxiliaries from provinces of the empire – this avoided the increase of the Roman legions. Italian legionnaires had an expectation upon retirement of being repatriated back to Italy. Auxiliaries upon retirement settled in their respective provinces.

The Dacian auxiliaries held their Draco standards with great respect. Draco standards grew in popularity, with slight variations. Some people called it the Scythian Draco. The Draco motif appeared on bracelets for men.

Lucy thought that it should be treated with respect because it meant so much to people and not stuck on the door of an apartment as a fun thing to frighten visitors.

*

Ndio's African Hercules

Ndio is in charge of the showroom, and unwrapping the new stock. She crosschecks each item adding one-hundred-per-cent to the cost price and placing small labels near the items with a brief description.

She looks at the black painted figures that have been created against the red Greek pottery. These artefacts are made in southern Italy. They are replicas – or even replicas of replicas – the original ones were rare and are never on sale, being such valuable collectors' items. Romans and tourists are keen to buy Greek ornaments.

Gently wiping away the packaging dust off the red kylix bowl in her hand, she looks at the flattish bowl with a handle on either side of the bowl, and supported on a single stem beneath standing on a flat disc-type base.

On the inside and outside of the flattish bowl a pottery artist had painted figures of satyrs. The mythical satyr figures have pointed ears a tail, like that of a horse or donkey, and small noses and the body being like that of a man. Around the outside edge of the bowl, the satyrs are playing flutes, dancing, and holding small containers of wine.

When first seeing a satyr painting, it embarrassed her looking at each creature with a large phallus or penis.

Ndio then reads that the satyr figures, or woodland creatures, would follow the god *Dionysus* whose father was *Zeus*, or known to the Romans as *Jupiter*, and his mother *Semele*, who was associated with the earth.

Dionysus was the god of fertility and wine, although he was never seen drinking wine. Ndio could not recall seeing any of the ancient sculptures of gods with enlarged sexual parts.

It was fun to discover the history of the gods and goddesses with their different clothing or items they would be seen holding to identify them, and try to remember which god was which, as there were so many gods and goddesses from Roman times and back into ancient times.

Opening another box, she picks up a small shelf-size statue of *Hercules*.

Not knowing about her childhood or where she came from, her friends in Rome said that she probably came from East Africa because she still had a little coloured bead bracelet, and she had used the word Ndio. They would tell her stories about East Africa to make her feel part of her original tribal life, although, like her, they did not know much their own past. Each possessing limited recollections of their places of origin. Her friends gave her the name Safiya.

They had told her about tribal life and that some chiefs wore a lion skin on their shoulders and carried a spear and a club. A chief, and the elders, were leaders who protected tribal people from dangers, and use spears to kill lions, or other wild animals to protect not only people and but their farm animals.

Inspecting the small statue of *Hercules* she begins to firmly believe that he must have come from Africa.

She remembered seeing a childhood book that Julia read for her schoolwork. *Hercules*, for his first labour had to kill a huge lion, which he did with his bare hands and arms. The statue in the showroom showed *Hercules* with a lion skin on his shoulder. Just like a tribal chief. With her soft dusting, she places him on the shelf with pride.

Next to the figurine, she places some grains in a small bowl as an offering to her little ornamental hero.

Her attention is drawn towards a man entering the showroom. He says that he wants to know the price of ebony-wood tables with gold on the bottom of the legs and at corners of the table top.

She asks for his present address and he gives the address of Sextus. Ndio says that Julia could visit him to tell him about sizes and prices.

'Have you just moved to Rome?'

'Well I'm originally from Scotland – but live in London. But would like to have a branch of my business here as well as an apartment in Rome.'

Ndio notices his dark reddish hair.

He wanders around the showroom and looks at the drinking mugs with humorous wording.

'I think I'll buy some of these to take back for my friends.'

'How long do you expect to stay?'

'Until about October. We hope to get away before the bad weather affects the sailing of ships on the Mediterranean.'

He looks at the mugs with humorous writing:

❀ ❀ ❀

I consecrate this wine to philosophy
May the wine and I never loose reasoning
Or is it reality?

❀ ❀ ❀

Women are fine
But draw the line
On perfumes and wine.

❀ ❀ ❀

You can take a seat
Enjoy the meat
But the wine on the table is mine.

❀ ❀ ❀

It is better to buy an old vineyard
And toast another man's hard work.

❀ ❀ ❀

'What's your name?'

'Ndio.'

'What does Ndio mean?' She explains how the situation arose.

'It just means 'yes.''

They both laugh.

As he is leaving the showroom, with one of each of the drinking mugs, he calls back to her.

'Well, Ndio-Yes-Yes, I will come into the showroom again and buy a few more things. I have enjoyed speaking with you.'

'Oh, everyone calls me Rufus because of my reddish hair – so you can call me Rufus. Now nobody knows our real names – but we know who we are!'

What a nice man she thought. But she did notice that he said 'we' and hopes that next time his wife would accompany him, as women buy more things than men.

Ndio felt very pleased with such a pleasant day. She gave a little impromptu dance of happiness. She could never become an unemotional stoic Roman citizen.

*

Lucy's problem

Upon entering Petrus' office, Lucy notices an olive wreath above the door, which indicates that he had won a legal case regarding property rights, Lucy feels anxious about discussing Crispus, as Petrus seems to be an important man. She wonders is Petrus will ask questions like Messalina? When he rose from his desk to greet her she could not stop glancing at him. They both look into each other's eyes and smile. There seems to be a mutual intimate moment of connection.

All the problems she had experienced these past twenty-four hours somehow seem to disappear.

Lucy tells him all about Julia's problem with Crispus.

Because Petrus has a kindly understanding face, she tells him a little about the poisoning of Marcus.

Petrus had known Marcus from school days. He had heard that Marcus was discretely learning to take over Sextus' business. Over time they would make contact again – both were busy men.

He promises Lucy that he will make a few discrete enquiries of his own about Crispus and his non-payment for the statue.

'I hope you can come back again soon. This is the best business meeting I have had all week.'

He places an arm on her shoulder as she begins to walk out through the door, and then stress overcomes her, causing tears to flow down her cheeks as she really feels in need of a little compassion. He holds her head close to his shoulder.

'Oh, I don't normally have this impact on people – you can poison me at any time – as long as you stay this close!'

She begins to smile a little.

'I don't think you should leave until you are relaxed from all the anxiety you have suffered.'

He leads her away from his office, into his adjoining house.

In the main drawing room are large sofas and cushions, panelled walls, and carpets placed on the marble floors. He has on top of a table a small display of carved ivory figurines depicting racing charioteers with horses.

As she begins to settle down, he brings over three of the figurines, explaining that they were of the charioteer Diocles who, years earlier, had won many chariot races. First Diocles represented the white team, then the green team, winning many races for each team, and finally the red team. She could see the colours painted on the figurines.

'I've never been to the races, but I love the figurines.'

'Lucy tells him all the details leading up to the poison which was intended for Sextus and how Marcus ate the cake.'

He begins to laugh as he visualises the scene – she laughs as well.

'It's no laughing matter. I still have to apologise to Sextus and Marcus.'

'Marcus will be all right – but I think Sextus will suffer from hurt pride just thinking about a pretty woman wanting to poison him'.

'Seems like you have had a few miserable hours.'

'Oh, that's not all. I had to visit Messalina.'

With that she related her dreadful experience of being cross questioned – by that time he was curling up with laughter, and they both saw the funny side.

'I am going to meet up with friends at the Circus Maximus races. Why don't you come us – and to make amends to Sextus, perhaps you can ask him if he will join us. When it's closer to the time I will collect you both.'

'I have never been to the races. Yes, I would like to thank you and will ask Sextus.'

He gave her a close brotherly hug as she departs.

Petrus is a wonderful man she thought.

*

As Marcus approaches Papinus house, there is a gardener sweeping the path with a homemade broom, made of twigs bunched around a long tree branch.

The gardener is looking miserable. He is missing Corinna's antics. Now there is no news going around for the chattering staff to discuss. Daily farm life seems quite boring.

Marcus gives a nod of greeting to the gardener and proceeds towards Papinus, who is sitting at a long wooden table with wooden chairs. The simple stone slab terrace is shaded with vines growing over a pergola.

Explaining the construction of the pergola, Papinus said: 'All the woodwork is made from local trees – all idyllic and rustic.'

They speak about the farm until Julia arrives and then all stroll towards the barn to look at the statue.

Just before entering the barn, one of the labourers had earlier placed an old sack for people to wipe their footwear before entering.

The barn, where Papinus keeps dried food storage, contains some vats of olives soaking in brine and *amphorae*, pottery containers, holding wine. There are also art materials that Papinus had purchased for Corinna, which she gave Tullio to use, but these had remained untouched.

Close to the barn is the old farmhouse, which is well furnished and comfortable, with locally made furniture, rugs and fabrics.

'The farm has been in the family for many, many years,' said Papinus. Over two hundred years ago, Emperor Augustus wanted to confiscate the farm, as he wanted to give family farms to retired soldiers who knew nothing about farming. My ancestors managed to negotiate and keep the farm, but each owner, in turn, is reminded of this by the sign on one of the rafters. 'This barn was made from trees planted by ancestors – remember with care.'

In the corner of the barn, balancing against supports is the copied statue of the *Victory*. The support upon which the statue rests, needs some slight repairs.

Papinus points to three marble garden benches he also wishes to sell. Marcus thinks they will look good by the pond area of Sextus' garden and said he will buy them.

There are two carved marble heads of ancient Greeks, *Odysseus* and *Poseidon*. Julia said that she would take them as well as the statue.

'Lycus, the captain, will be very happy to receive the statue and the two busts. We need some form of packaging to get them down to the river Tiber and onto boats to reach the coast before boarding a larger vessel. I am sure Lycus will arrange the journey on one of his three ships,' said Marcus.

'Wrapping and packaging for the carvings can be handled by my farm labourers,' replied Papinus.

When they left Papinus handed them a package. Inside were two farm mulberry pies and a pot of cream.

On their return journey, Marcus asks Julia to speak with Lucy and Petrus about travelling together down to Capri.

*

Letter to Capri

Marcus writes a long letter to Captain Lycus saying that he can obtain a smaller copy of the statue of the winged *Victory*. It is about the height of a man, but the pedestal is slightly damaged. The statue belongs to his friend Papinus. It is made from marble that is found on the Greek island of Paros, which is translucent, and then brought to southern Italy, where Greek marble craftsmen had made this great carving.

On the letter scroll he draws a picture of the statue of the goddess standing on the prow of a ship. The base has a little damaged, he explains.

Lycus, having been a captain on merchant ships for many years, has always been interested in collecting carvings that related to the gods and myths, and especially if they are connected to the protection of seafarers and their ships.

Ancient mariners have always taken heed of warnings or signals given by birds or fish, predicting the arrival of poor weather conditions. Mariners take heed to these warnings and make small offerings to their gods for safety at sea.

He told the captain the names of the people who will accompany him, and that they will travel down the Tiber River, to Ostia and hopefully travel on one of his vessels. They would like to spend a couple of nights with him in Capri before returning to Rome.

*

Slaves sometimes believe themselves cleverer than their masters

Crispus' maid, a friend of Ndio, pops into the showroom.

'My Madam is going on holiday to visit her brother in France, and she is taking me with her.'

'How long will you be away?'

'I don't know, but I think it will be around a month.'

'Who will be staying in the property?'

'Just the boss, Crispus. There is a watchman who regularly checks up on the house at midnight. He has a manservant and a cleaner, but they also work at a smaller property which Crispus owns and sleep at the smaller property.'

'I'm the only slave, who sleeps there and the cook, an elderly man.' She pauses then proudly says, 'I've now been promoted to being Madam's dresser and look after her clothes, and hair.'

Some time back, she had told Ndio that she was sold as a slave. It was a time when Septimius Severus and his legions were fighting a civil war against the Roman commander Niger in Asia Minor. Severus won and any town which supported Niger had several of its the people taken as slaves, or killed.

She was just sixteen and her father had promised her in marriage to the son of his distant cousin. The young man lived in a small town that was under attack from the Romans, as was her own town.

Sadly, her family were killed. She was captured by soldiers and sold on as a slave, and along with other captured people she was taken to Rome.

I am glad you have a better job taking care of your madam, but I will miss you – hopefully you'll be back soon?'

Crispus' maid had previously told Ndio that Crispus bought her when she was being sold by a trader, who had placed a board around her neck, saying "sex slave". This custom was acceptable by Roman law.

Owners would use these women as low paid workers but would be entitled to sleep with them or use them as a form of income. If they produced children, then the offspring increased the owner's workforce. Crispus fancied a number of slave children all being girls, but his wife put a stop to that idea.

The minute Crispus' wife found out that her maid was pregnant she took her off for an abortion. A lot of Roman women had abortions and Madam did not want to see a nursery of boys looking just like her husband, or worse still a girl looking like her husband.

The maid had told Ndio, that Madam liked having her hair designed in tiny curls at the front and sides, and longish at the back. Of course, she often got a beating if a hairclip jabbed Madam's head when she quickly turned her head, or a beating if a broach was the wrong one for her cloak.

But Madam had her good points because she had allowed her to sleep outside her bedroom door. Whenever Crispus tried to drag her away for sex, she would pretend to be on the verge of vomiting. Madam hearing her make such noises would come out of her bedroom, and bring her into her bedroom to sleep on the floor inside the room.

'Going with the Madam was better than being left behind with the Crispus.' Ndio nodded in agreement.

When she left the showroom she said, 'I wish I had a life like you – working for a good family.'

Now alone in the showroom, Ndio realises that she has a good employer and, placing a duster under each foot, she skates around the marble floor in the showroom, to keep off the dust and make it clean and shiny, humming a little tune to herself to keep time with her leg movement.

*

Marcus decides that it would be good manners to speak with Julia's father about the journey to Capri with his daughter Julia and Lucy. Quintus is Lucy's guardian whilst she lives in Rome and her parents live in France.

He explains to the Senator their journey, taking with them the statue and two busts. 'I think you need to take Petrus. You will need at least two men and some slaves.

'Julia has agreed to speak with Petrus and with Lucy.'

'My uncle Sextus has some workers at the warehouses on the dockside at Ostia, and one or two can take the journey with us and carry the statue, busts, and our belongings.

'I'm hoping that the Captain will arrange for us to travel in one of his ships, and we will be given a couple of cabins, so that the girls can share one.

'We intend to rest for one or two days in Capri, then return partly up the Italian coast, and partly by road.'

'I have some friends living in that area,' said the senator. 'They live near Terracina. I will tell Gundher to write to them to expect your arrival. You can discuss details with him.'

'Thank you, sir.'

'I've known you all your life Marcus although we only rarely meet. Your uncle Sextus and I go back a long way as friends. I know that you have been made to learn his business from the bottom up. He wants you to find any weakness in the business before he handed it over to you. But have you told my daughter who you are?'

'Well, I'm still supposed to keep myself anonymous – do you think I should tell her now?'

'Yes, she deserves to know – because if she finds out later she will not be able to trust you.'

'Then I will tell her before we depart. Thank you, sir, for your advice.'

'However, there is another matter – it's about Julia's business,' comments Marcus. 'She is relying on the showroom for her business – and two of the main customers are Sextus, and Elagabalus.

'I would like your opinion first on my idea for a business plan I could put to her.

'For example she could buy items in larger quantities. Italian objects, such as beautiful Italian glassware, jewellery, and ready-made panels of mosaics with zodiac, or animal signs. Also, paintings showing fruits, birds and gardens.

'Buying these in bulk at a lower price from the makers, which she can export to different agents in the coastal regions or provinces, will bring her in a better return and improve her business.

'We already have several warehouses for shipping, but she needs to organize packaging, buying and selling.'

Quintus replies, 'Please speak with Julia, and come back to me again about taking this forward.'

Marcus thought about the Senator's ideas, but the problem was speaking about it with Julia.

*

Messalina's quest to win friends.

Messalina did not like to have her meeting with Julia cancelled, especially for Papinus whom she hardly knows and he was not one of the names listed in her diary.

In her daily appointments, she wrote: "Today am going to visit Papinus" and the previous entry above it said, "I am very disappointed that Julia made an excuse not to come. I had biscuits waiting for each of us to eat together. I think that she lied and just wanted to stay in the showroom. Lucy was not very convincing. Have put her biscuit back in the cupboard. It ruined my day".

She did not employ a maid. She has basic cooking facilities and buys from food shops.

Cleaning work in her building, such as staircases, windows and corridors, is carried out by the maintenance workers, employed by the owners of the building.

Messalina notices that her apartment floors are not looking quite as shiny as she wishes them to look – admittedly she has walked on them for several days. She asks one of the building cleaners to privately clean her floors, and she will reward him later.

Picking up her small shopping bag, she walks down the street to the intersection. Ignoring the people in the queue who wish to hire litters she goes to the front and demands to hire a chair-type litter that is carried on the shoulders of two men, to take her to Papinus' farm dwelling.

They are instructed to wait for her.

Walking towards his house, Papinus' headman, Felix, meets her at the entrance gate and asks if she had been invited to the house by Papinus, if so she could sit on the terrace and wait. He offers to bring her something to drink.

'No.' She moves away. She never says "thank you" to lowly workers. She walks further away, dismissing him.

Approaching the vegetable and herb patch she wanders in and out looking for what she can pick to take home. Well there is lavender, but perhaps there is something to take home and eat.

'Please take care - we have planted a lot of seedlings,' says Felix.

Messalina is not going to be told by a slave where she can and cannot walk.

He stands, watching her from a distance. He has never seen her before and he knows that his master will be cross if he lets strangers wander around.

It was an old family farm. There were some fruit trees planted by older family members, and there is a section where Papinus lets the workers plant trees and crops for their families.

Some of the elderly workers often take Papinus' vegetable and fruits to the market outside the city walls, alongside some of their own produce. Over time they all formed a close unit. Their families and Papinus' family had all worked in harmony for many years.

The farm manager knows that Papinus likes to walk around every plant and tree – and if the weather is good he takes a stroll further to check on the animals in the fields. He knows all his animals by name, even the ducks. His old dog will lazily get up from outside the barn and walk practically leg to leg with his master.

The dog shows his disapproval of Messalina with the odd gruff and never letting his eyes move away from her. He was also watching the manager's reaction and awaiting an order whether to act as friendly pet or guard dog – his ears are up and listening.

She decides to pick handfuls of lavender. It will make nice posies for the women to wear on their shoulders with the clasps on their dresses – or on their belts with ribbons. Not caring whether Papinus needs the plants – they are hers for the picking. Yet these plants have been cultivated to sell at the market.

These little gifts, she believes, will make her the centre of attention when she attends the event in the showroom.

As she walks towards the fruit trees the assistant manager steps in front of her. 'Let me help carry your basket,' which has now been loaded with lavender.

'I think you must sit and wait for the master to return.'

'How dare you try to stop me from collecting lavender.'

She had planned to look at the fruit trees and take some fruit home.

'I am going to report you to the civic guards and have you arrested for preventing a woman of my good Roman birth from...'

He began to walk towards her litter with the lavender, saying: 'Madam, you are taking my bosses plants. He has not told me that you have permission.'

'Move - out of my way! You should be beaten and taken to prison for your insolence. Remember you are a slave.'

'I am a freedman and farm manager.'

'Well to me you are still a slave.' With that she marched off to her litter.

When Papinus returned, Felix told him the story.

'You were doing the right thing – I will speak with my friend Petrus in Rome and ask him for advice. But first we will see if she takes any further action.'

*

Crispus on the cusp of cornucopia

Petrus wonders how to meet Crispus in a casual manner, on the pretext of gaining some knowledge as to Crispus' financial situation. He decides that the best place for this encounter is the public baths, where Crispus likes to attend every day.

It is going to be difficult to create a conversation about Crispus' garden sculpture, especially since Petrus had never seen it. But he is making the effort so that he can see Lucy again.

But suddenly, Crispus appears at the door of his office looking pale like a man who had stepped barefoot on a hedgehog.

'Today I received a message by courier from my father's farm manager, saying that my father is in poor health and likely to die. I must go and see him.

'I want to speak with you about his Will, which I have not seen yet, but the farm manager is holding it until I arrive.'

Petrus could see that this overweight man was out of breath and orders a servant to bring him a glass of wine with plenty of water.

'My father has a close relationship with a local woman who owned a tavern. In recent years she sold her business and moved in with him. But I'm worried in case my elderly father married her. Hopefully she has not borne him any male children. I have not had time to visit him these past years. We just send messages.'

'Does she communicate with you?'

'No, the news comes from the farm manager. My father owns three small farms.'

'My father sends me regular amounts of money from his farms, and I have always felt that when he dies that I will inherit everything. But now I am quite worried. I shall have to make arrangements to see just how sick he is.'

Petrus said, 'I suggest that you quickly send a courier with a letter to the farm manager. Tell him that you are making arrangments to see your father as quickly as possible. State your intentions that should your father die before your arrival, you intend to continue using him as manager in charge of the house and farms. This should at least keep him happy, and for him to use his discretion regarding the tavern lady.'

'I'll do that straight away.'

'I am sure that you will be able to handle your father's Will in the town near to where he lives, but please keep in touch with me should you need help.'

Crispus was indeed worried as he makes his way home. He walks like a puppet when the puppet master has loosened the strings, with his head down and his arms and legs ceasing to be in harmony. He needs regular money but there could be a problem if his father has married the tavern women, it could leave him with less money. Then he worries in case she has run up lots of debt.

He vows that if he inherits everything from his father, from that moment, he will vow to be faithful to his wife and not secretly remove and sell her silver ornaments.

After leaving Petrus, he returns to his house to pack for the farms in Umbria. He makes his way to his atrium in the centre of the house where he has a small altar, and in earlier times had place a little figurine of *Plutus*, the god of wealth, who holds a cornucopia. He tells his small god image – 'I am placing in your cornucopia a little offering of wine

with the hope that you bring me bountiful wealth.'
He then drinks a great deal to help him control his
anxiety.

He finds a note on a table from his wife, saying
that she has left with her maid, for a holiday in
France and she will be staying with her brother.

Crispus remembers that he will be attending
Julia's showroom event, and sends a message to
Messalina to say that he will meet her there. He
will find the right time to tell her about his journey
and his father.

Messalina is his only loyal friend who enjoys
consuming sumptuous meals with masses of
oysters and unusual birds and fish on the menu.
There is no sexual attraction on his part.

Re-reading the farm manager's letter, he
notices that the tavern lady has been told to leave
the farm immediately, because the farm manager
thought it will avoid a difficult situation when
Crispus arrives.

The manager's actions were appropriate,
because he does not wish to arrive and find the
tavern woman controlling the household servants
and his father's possessions, whilst he is left to feel
like an interloper.

Following Petrus' instructions he sends a courier back with a message saying that he will leave very early in the morning.

Later in the day, Papinus speaks with Petrus about Messalina wandering around his farm. Petrus tells him that it would be a waste of time to challenge her over the lavender. Just mention, in a friendly way, that she must only visit the farm when invited, because the farm manager has to be informed in advance.

CHAPTER FOUR

The Self-Interest of Emperor Elagabalus

The Senator leaves a note for Gundher to make arrangements for Julia, Lucy, Petrus and Marcus to stay with his friends on their return journey when passing through Terracina.

Gundher has on many occasions written letters on the senator's behalf, and knows the normal procedure for arranging compatible dates and times.

On a separate note, is a further instruction to Gundher. 'While Julia is absent, you will be in charge of the business, with Ndio helping in the showroom. Report back to me, discretely, if there are any problems.' Gundher knows that the senator does not wish to show himself as being involved in any commercial enterprise.

Gundher tells Ndio the news and that he will be in charge, but suggested that perhaps this will be a perfect time for them to buy a cheap statue, like the *Venus* which Crispus has in his garden, but this replacement will be extremely cheap. They could then swop expensive *Venus*-1 for inexpensive *Venus*-2. If Crispus does not pay his bill, then they have only made a loss on the cheap version Venus-2. They can sell the more expensive one at a later date. However, if he does pay then they will discretely return the expensive statue.

'Sounds complicated. But I like the idea,' Ndio replies.

'But we need a wagon to move the statues.'

'What about using the senator's old gardener at the house, he often drives a mule wagon?'

'It can't be done in the daytime', replies Gundher, 'because wheeled vehicles are not allowed – so we will go in the evening. We don't want to be recognised either. We will disguise ourselves as elderly people like the gardener.'

'So how do we start?'

'Well I will get the copy of the cheaper *Venus*-2, and you can store it in the back of the storeroom. When Julia and Lucy go down to Capri we can swop it one evening.'

Ndio says, 'I am friendly with the Crispus' maid and she told me that the Madam is travelling to France, and that her boss Crispus sleeps like a log.'

They are unaware that Crispus is about to visit his father.

*

Plans for Capri – Marcus faces Julia's wrath

Marcus walks enthusiastically towards the showroom. He is excited to speak with Julia about their visit to Capri, and the idea of increasing her business. With a little diplomacy he hopes to broach the subject that Sextus is his uncle, also explaining that he has been working undercover for business purposes.

Whilst plucking up courage to say the right things, he strolls passed a ladies' clothing store, with a few maids waiting around for their madam's instructions to hold the parcels. Then passes a man's clothing store selling togas for important people. He can see a crimson one with gold, for the generals, and one with a large purple stripe, and narrower still for equestrians. He can see capes and cloaks, expensive sandals and other styles of foot-ware, all very expensive. Then meets Julia.

Julia is not happy to see him.

Without even greeting him – she looks angry. 'I'm glad you are here. I recall telling you, when you went to see my client Sextus, *not* to alter the plans and design. I find out that you went ahead with your own ideas!'

'Well, there is something I would like to tell you ...'

Before he can finish she puts the palm of her hand towards his face to cut him short.

Her reprimand continues. 'You do not work for this company. You were given the task because you ruined my drawings,' she pauses.

He waits.

'You did not stick to the drawings nor my instructions. Fortunately for you, the customer, Sextus, likes the new idea of the pond with statues of *Diana* and the nymphs. And a wooden carving of *Acteon* and woodland carved animals amongst the trees and a bench.'

'Can I explain?'

'No!'

'I don't want you to go to Sextus' house again. Leave this to Lucy and me. Gundher can order the sculptures of *Diana*, the nymphs and the hounds. It is better if you stick to what you know - the theatre.'

He had a feeling that the business was rather worrying her. This did not seem the time to tell her that he lived in the same house as Sextus.

Well he did promise her father to tell her the truth, but it was more difficult than anticipated.

'I came to bring you the good news about the plans for Capri.'

Marcus tells Julia that he had received a reply from the Captain, saying that he urgently requires the items as he has just built a sunroom with windows, and doors that open out to face the sea, which is where he would like to position the statue. He tells her that Lycus is a collector of items that are associated with the sea, ancient mariners and myths.

Lycus also confirmed that he will arrange for a ship at Ostia to take them to the island of Capri.'

'I look forward to meeting Lycus,' replies Julia.

'Oh, by the way,' she slightly cocks her head to one side with a smile on her face – 'Would you like to come to my showroom event – I will send you the details.'

'I should like that – but ...'

With that she disappears from view.

*

Roman Emperor Elagabalus, rites, and performance.

Quintus is feeling a little insecure about Julia's dealings with Elagabalus. The senator owns two large farms and had never worked in commerce nor been a trader. Quintus finds it difficult to understand verbal agreements, made on trust that passes between businessmen, often without written documentation.

He wonders whether Julia should trust Elagabalus and if it would have been better to have a written agreement in advance regarding payment for her work.

Julia, probably, must find her own experience in the business world, he decides, but it does not stop him from worrying.

He met with his friend Dio for a mid-day meal. The senator makes Elagabalus the central point of discussion, but pointing out to his friend that the emperor is not like earlier emperors such as Trajan or Hadrian.

Dio says, 'Elagabalus mainly dresses in a long-sleeved tunic that comes down to the lower part of his legs. From his waist to the ends of his toes he wears leggings. His clothing is decorated in purple and gold with many precious stones, and he likes to wear jewellery and necklaces and on his face rouge, lipstick and eye make-up. You would never see Trajan wearing such clothes.

'I realise that he's just a pubescent boy with a lot thrust upon him. Obviously, he is unable to control a large empire and the legions. Yet, he appears to treat his role as if he is an actor carrying out a performance with an audience. Unable to take on the responsibility as head of the empire.'

'I agree,' says the senator. 'Elagabalus, prior to becoming an emperor in Rome was called Varius Avitus Bassianus. Upon becoming emperor he was called Marcus Aurelius Antoninus Augustus. But now he has given himself the title: 'The Most Magnificent Priest of the Invincible Sun Elagabalus.'

'Regardless of the hierarchy of nouns, or names, we will just stick to simply calling the emperor, Elagabalus,' replies Dio.

The senator continues, 'In the senate, because his grandmother has instructed him to dress in accordance with the rules of the senate, he appears wearing Roman robes, except his are of pure silk, which is considered to be the type of fabric suitable for women to wear. It is not the way he desires to dress, preferring his eastern, elaborate, and bejewelled clothing. It is this falseness – where he pretends to dress like all the previous emperors, but wants to mock the formal wear.

'Just imagine if all the senators follow suit, all wearing Chinese silk clothing. Silk is acceptable if mixed with other fabrics, but not pure silk. The next thing is that some would want to change the colour of white to pink or, worse still, yellow.' They laugh at such a thought.

'On occasions, when parading his god, Elagabaal, through the streets, he clothes himself in his eastern priestly robes. Nobody objects to his priestly clothing, and being adorned with jewellery and escorted by the cavalry, priests, soldiers, senators, various other dignitaries, and statues of gods and goddesses. It is the spectacle that people enjoy, and it takes their mind off their everyday cares. Yet they seem not to realise that the emperor also has the ability to improve their existence, and not have them grasping at handouts, parades and millions spent on spectacles to keep them from objecting to the poorer lifestyles in which they live,' comments Dio.

'Elagabalus enjoys the illusion of his baetyl god on a carriage holding the reigns as if the god is in charge of the six white horses pulling the carriage. Both carriage and horses are bedecked with gold and jewels.

'In order to achieve this apparition, the emperor manages to run backwards, whilst bridles are held in is hands, yet not taking his eyes off his god in the carriage, causing the crowds watch in amazement. The emperor has no frontal vision, but to aid him, a trail of gleaming white sand has been laid down on the road ahead so that he can use this as a line of direction.'

'Pedestrians and other onlookers line the streets and throw flowers.

'When the temple rituals are finished he ascends a tower and throws down clothing, and other items to the crowds below, as well as gold and silver,' says the senator.

The conversation between Dio and the senator drifted towards ancient rituals. 'I think most ancient beliefs relate to rituals and performance,' the senator points out.

'For example, we both attended the celebrations of the Great Mother, Magna Mater, who goes back to primordial times as the mother of the gods. Earlier this year we celebrated the Great Mother. There are many images of this ancient goddess depicted in many shapes in carvings and pottery and stone, around the Greece and Asia Minor.

'Magna Mater also came in the form of a small black sacred meteorite that had come down to earth, and later incorporated in a human shaped sculpture. In Crete she was known as the goddess Cybele.

'Magna Mater, or Cybele, now has a sculptured human body and is accompanied by lions, one on each side.

Priests are called *galli*, inferring that a priest is neither a man nor a woman. The *galli* are only able to carry out work that related to the temple, and begging for money and food. Aristocrats help to support them.'

'Around sixty years ago,' reflects Dio, 'the senate allowed the castration of animals instead of the castration of humans. Magna Mater's ancient rites were different from other rites, in that Attis, her consort, had castrated himself as his devotion to her – and all the devotees act accordingly.

'Elagabalus makes sure that it is the duty of all senators to attend the remembrance ceremony for the ancient goddess - including the presence of the equestrian order. As you know, we are all made to stand around according to rank and clothed according to the emperor or high priest's instructions.

'Chosen prefects and officials wear long-sleeved Phoenician tunics, shoes of linen – being clothing as dictated by the priests. Anyone who chooses to criticise can be executed.'

The senator reasons, 'Elagabalus, as *pontifex maximus,* head of the temples of Rome, appears to enjoy his role when initiates are placed in pits beneath a perforated board. A bull and a sheep are slaughtered on the board, and their blood drains through the holes onto the heads of the initiates below.

'At the altar, entrails and spices are mixed with certain parts of the carcases and testicles and placed in golden bowls. Chosen senior officials from the senate and military prefects in their long robes are honoured by carrying these golden bowls for presentation to the goddess Magna Mater.

'Devotees flagellate themselves and toss their heads back and forth, which Elagabalus as priest encourages his followers to join in the dancing with music and cymbals, flutes and drums, and enjoys himself.

'Certain parts of the meat, from the animal carcases, goes to the priests and the rest of the meat is for the people.'

*

The conversation moves from the young emperor's performance to his private married life. Dio comments, 'I am amazed that Elagabalus wants to produce a godlike child, when marrying a young Vestal virgin, but has shown lack of virility with any of his wives in producing any offspring.

'His first marriage had been arranged by his grandmother, soon after his arrival. Probably, to connect him with Roman aristocracy, as well as improve his credentials in society.

'Julia Cornelia Paula who was his first bride was celebrated by all in Rome, but after all the expensive celebrations, he divorced her on the grounds of a blemish. Taking away her dignity – or should I say having no respect for the young woman.'

'He behaved in a disgraceful manner with his second marriage, because he violated the sacral laws and rites laid down for the behaviour of a Vestal Virgin,' said the senator.

Dio continues, 'I think he disrespected Roman history and the ancient custom of keeping the temple fire burning. Young girls between the ages of six to ten years of age are generally picked from aristocratic families.

'The custom is that a girl is selected by a Vestal Priest, and is taken away from her own father's protection and then placed under the influence and control of the temple *pontifex*. She is housed in the temple's quarters, for use by women.

'The minimum time spent as a Vestal Virgin is for five years, but a woman can stay for thirty years, but she must remain a virgin for life. The history of this ancient belief goes back to the time when the goddess, Vesta, made a promise to keep the hearth and fire alight for Rome, and that she will remain a virgin.

'This ancient tradition has continued in Rome from the time of the second king of Rome, BCE 715-672, when the formation of priestly colleges began. The failure of duty by the virgins can result in some form of punishment such as being whipped.

'If a Vestal Virgin breaks the rule of chastity she is to be buried alive.

'Elagabalus, sullied this purity by taking the Vestal Virgin, Julia Aquila Severa, from the woman's quarters to become his second wife. When he was made to give his reason to the senate, he claimed that he was overcome with 'manly passion.'

The senator said, 'He wants the public to find approval in his actions – even believing that he can produce a god-like child.'

'What action could the senate take against the emperor?' It was a rhetorical question - he did not expect and answer.

'His next quest,' said Dio, 'was to find an ideal goddess wife for his meteorite god.

'Ancient Phoenician settlers of Carthage, Tunis, and Libya, had worshipped the goddess Urania. The goddess was also associated with the ancient moon goddess, Astarte of Asia Minor.

'The emperor had already deprived the worshippers in Syria of their god Elagabaal, when the meteorite was taken to Rome, but this did not deter him from demanding to remove, from those worshippers in North Africa, their goddess Urania.

'He also requested from the temple in Carthage, the accompanying golden lions which were positioned on either side of the goddess, and to provide a marriage dowry. He melted down the gold lions soon after arrival in Rome.'

The senator believes that Elagabalus is heading down a slippery slope. 'Elagabalus then gave thought to the Greek goddess, *Athena*. Maybe she will be a suitable wife for his god. Then had second thoughts, because Elagabaal may not like to have a wife that is also a goddess of war.

'But it not deter him from his efforts to obtain items or artefacts connected with ancient Greek history which were stored in the temple in Rome to be taken to the new temple of Elagabaal. The emperor's interest lay in possessing the fire from the Temple of Vesta, as well as the Palladium.

'It is said that the Palladium, being in the form of a thinly carved idol supposedly sent down from heaven by the god Zeus, was believed to be a wooden image of Pallas, that had been carved by Athena. According to the Roman writer, Virgil, in his story the *Aeneid*, the artefact was sacred and that whichever country possessed this item would never lose in war.

'It had been in the hands of the Trojans, but when they were about to lose the battle, it was saved by *Odysseus*. Virgil in his book relating to the founding of Rome, introduces the Trojan king *Priam*'s son, *Aeneas*, and the journey made by his followers to Rome and the arrival of the Palladium, which Elagabalus wants to possess.

'Elagabalus, ignored the Roman historic value of the Palladium. However, he was unaware that the item was placed in one of two identical pots. He chose the wrong one.'

Dio is getting carried away with the arrogance of Elagabalus wishing to remove items from Roman temples. 'Elagabalus wants to take artefacts that the Roman people hold close to their hearts, which have historical value, going back to the second ruler of Rome, King Numa.

'He desired to remove the Ancile shield. This is believed to be a magic shield, oval in shape, and cut away at the sides to allow arm movement. In history it goes back in time to the 12 dancing priests (the Salii). The shield was lying secure in the temple on Palatine hill.   But unknown to

Elagabalus, the king had made several copies, and the young emperor took a copied shield.'

The Senator says, 'I do not think he respects Roman women either. He is now into his third marriage. His new wife Annia Faustina had been married to Pomponius Bassus, and she bore two young children. This family was broken up when her husband was killed on the orders of the emperor, on unidentified charges of subversive activities.

'A few months later Elagabalus married this extremely wealthy widow, who came from the long line of Nerva and Antonine descendants. She was instructed by Elagabalus never to mention her husband nor mourn him. Even though only a year before her marriage to Elagabalus she had given birth to Pomponius Bassius' son. Elagabalus did not stay married long to Annia Faustina, this being his third marriage to come to an end in a short time.'

*

Lanterns and moonlight

Rufus is walking around the Forum looking at temples and writing notes and making sketches on a small scroll. Papinus is on his way to the library when he notices Rufus, and asks if he is a tourist.

'Yes, and no. I design lamps for terraces, patios, and gardens. At present I am looking for ideas for decorations. I am from London but am planning to set up a branch of my business here in Rome.'

'What designs have you found so far?'

'I have been looking at the Corinthian acanthus leaves on the top of the columns, and also the Ionic scroll designs on the temple capitals. Such as shown on the Temple of *Castor* and *Pollux* and the Temple of *Saturn*. All of these, on a much smaller scale and in a simplified design, would look good for my metal garden lamps.

'Perhaps you would like to know that the twins, *Castor* and *Pollux*, had twin sisters, one being Helen of Troy and the other *Clytemnestra* who was the wife of King *Agamemnon*. I do not know whether you remember the story Helen of Troy and the Trojan War?'

'It was a long time ago when I read it, but will have to read it again now that you have mentioned these names.'

Rufus notices that Papinus is about thirty-five years of age, the same as himself, yet he appears older, possibly because he was very thin with longish hair.

Papinus asks, 'Where are you staying in Rome?'

'I am staying one or two nights with Sextus and Marcus. I am trying to look for an apartment to buy and some place to store my goods, prior to selling them to the proprietors of shops or market stalls.'

'I know Sextus and Marcus well,' Papinus remarks. 'Come over to my farmhouse and join me for lunch. I will show you my barn where you can store a few things until you get yourself established. Petrus, a friend, deals with properties to buy and rent and I will introduce you to him when you are ready.

'The other temple that you looked at, the Temple of *Saturn*, holds the state's treasury. In December the image of the ancient god *Saturn* is brought out of the temple – following which the people relax and enjoy themselves. Hopefully you will stay in Rome for December.'

'You make it sound interesting.'

'Come, let's go to my farm. You are welcome to rent my small farm house whilst you are looking around for the right premises, and you can store your things in the barn – there is plenty of space.'

'I should mention that I have my sister Anna, who is also with me,' says Rufus.

'Would love to meet her.'

'My sister and I would like, in the future, to come to Rome for a few weeks each year to check on the business and have a branch here.'

'My headman is called Felix. It is his duty to organise everything on the farm. Just tell him of your routine, and he will sort everything out.'

'Perhaps I may get some ideas after looking at the plants around your farm,' comments Rufus.

'You might enjoy the clear evenings on the farm, where the starry nights and constellations may also provide you with ideas for your lanterns,' says Papinus.

'I can't wait to visit your farm – I shall bring Anna later in the day to meet you.'

*

At cross purposes

It is time for the showroom event. Messalina looks around to see if Crispus is present and whether he has brought his wife, whom she believes to be snooty and aloof.

Using her little bouquets of lavender allows her the opportunity to go up to people and give them a few flowers. They thanked her for these small gifts.

Papinus notices that Messalina keeps looking around to see if he notices her – she wants to cause a scene and complain about his farm worker. He decides not to give her the opportunity, as he had heard stories that Messalina likes to use people for her own ends, such as expecting people to cut her hair for free or expecting people to carry out small jobs, but having no intention of doing any work for others.

It was not that she is poor, she just likes to control people in her small way. She is reluctant to part with her money, hoping others would pay for items. Her conversations of friendship often began, 'I wonder if you can do me a favour ...'

Papinus has no intention of being used by Messalina or encouraging her to become part of his lifestyle.

The day before attending the gathering she decided to ask a friend to accompany her to the other side of the Tiber so that she could rummage amongst the second-hand goods in the market. She purchased a second-hand shawl, assuming that it had previously belonged to a wealthy equestrian's wife, or senator's wife. It is this latest purchase that she is wearing at the showroom. She is hoping someone will comment about how good she looks, and with such flair.

Her cloak or shawl has an abundance of embroidery on the edges, and tiny rubies dotted around, and she hopes that Crispus will notice her appearance.

Messalina stuck some pieces of lavender in her hair. She flirts with Crispus, offering him titbits of food, as well as gossip.

However, she is caught off-guard when Crispus announces the news that he is leaving Rome in a few hours' time to visit his father. Her attempts to taunt Papinus, and lavender incident, all fade away.

His wife comes from an old aristocratic family, and it became a challenge for Messalina to try and make his wife jealous of her relationship with Crispus. She keeps speaking in low tones to him or whispering in his ear to try and break up his relationship with his wife. She enjoys causing disharmony and rifts amongst friends and their families.

He barely notices that she is flirting – eating his snacks with no enjoyment. He is thinking about his father and whether the old man has married the tavern woman, and whether the old man signed any of his money to her in his old age unknowingly.

He cannot reveal his problems to Messalina, because she will tell every one of his friends and neighbours.

Crispus is thinking about his father's impending demise, and beginning to visualise himself as becoming one of the landed gentry.

Should he become the sole heir, he will take on the image of an important man, lounging around in a fine carriage, being the honoured as an invited guest at dinner parties and being served the choicest meat and fish servings.

Messalina could not be one of his hangers-on because most of the men he knows, when he attended important dinner functions, do not like sitting next to her as she talks about her marvels holidays in Athens and the conversation is always about herself. Otherwise she grows bored very quickly and will try and change the subject when others were enjoying a conversation of joint interest.

Crispus was quietly mumbling to himself, and she hears him utter something about the slaves on the farm.

Messalina decides to join in when she hears the word 'slaves', and relates it to her own problem earlier that day.

'I asked one of the slave workers, employed by the property owners, whose job is to clean the corridors, staircases and remove the trash, in the building, if he will carry out a private bit of work, to clean my floors in the apartment.

'He agrees because he thinks it will provide him with a little extra cash or a gift. I know what he wants in return, but had fun pretending not to understand. Upon completion of the work, he expects his reward.

'I call him to my apartment, to where I have a collection of tourist scrolls from Egypt. I present him with a scroll of a pyramid.'

'He left the apartment in a huff - slaves are always ungrateful, always expecting money.'

Now Crispus had her full attention. Not because of what she said, but because he realises he must make haste to his father's farms.

'I am thinking that I may employ a senior slave who can sort out my accounts, book appointments, contact friends, to arrange holidays, so that I can stay with them. I hate writing letters. An important man, such as myself, cannot spend his time on trivial matters.'

Messalina retorts: 'Well I still think that it's their own fault if they became slaves. They can't expect special treatment. After all, I don't pay my friends when they help assist with some work.

'Aristotle, was reported to have said something to the effect that a slave does not have reasoning power – and that's the difference. I have reasoning – I know the slave will come back and expect more work from me.'

He failed to notice that she was speaking.

'I will be away for a few days.'

'Shall I keep an eye on your property?'

'No, Petrus or his staff will take care of the property.'

Crispus does not want her wandering around his premises on the pretext that she is acting as the manager on his behalf. She is just a companion to enjoy meals with – otherwise totally irrational and erratic to be put in charge of anything.

She is disappointed because she wants to feel needed – but on the other hand she has no intention of trying to find time in her diary to keep an eye on his property. That was more of a duty rather than a frivolous outing.

Messalina consults her diary, to impress him. 'Oh, it seems that I shall be staying with friends when you are away.' At the same time she was quickly jotting down on her tablet a fictitious appointment. 'So, can you make a date to meet up when you return?'

He just ate on not noticing what he was eating. He had eaten some of his food but left the hens' feet which had decorations made by the cook so that the hens' toenails were painted black.

How many bread rolls does it take to make a man satisfied, she wonders? She makes sure that she takes more than she can eat. Then, as usual, she takes portions home with her, to offer to her visitors.

*

Gundher and Julia go to meet Elagabalus at the palace to show him sketches and ideas for his water feature. He approves Julia's plans for a fountain with water trickling down to a small pond.

'I would like the bottom of the pond and the sides to be in black marble, so that the water looks clear.'

She suggested different types of statues around the side of the pond, but believes that he will choose the one of *Narcissus*.

'Here are some designs for statues, perhaps you may find the one or two statues of *Narcissus* suitable. The first one shows the god lying flat on the ground next to a pond with his head over the side peering into the water. Another is showing him leaning on one arm as he rests at the side of the pond, and leaning over to look at a clear reflection of himself.'

'I like the last one.'

'We will also place some little narcissus flowers in little areas around the pond, and some water lilies in the pond.'

Gundher asks, 'Where will the pond be positioned?'

Elagabalus was walking away and turning to Julia says, 'I shall be attending the races fairly soon and I will show you the place for the pond on that occasion.

'You are invited to come as my guest to the races, and please bring a friend. On the day of the races, before entering the track, in the grounds of the palace, I will show you the Septizodium, which is where the pond will be positioned.'

'After the races finish, you and your guest can join me, and my other guests, at the palace.'

'Thank you – I will look forward to that'.

CHAPTER FIVE

Circus Maximus - the Emperor's trophy Hierocles

Elagabalus meets with Marcus and Julia at the palace. Accompanied by his guards, they walk along to the Septizodium, a water feature that had been designed by Septimius Severus.

The Septizodium façade consists of three-storey-high columns, with water running down the niches and collecting temporarily in a water basin at the bottom, then circulating the water back up to the top line a continuous waterfall.

The emperor shows Julia the area where his pond is to be constructed, slightly further away from the Septizodium. Choosing a quiet spot where he can sit in peace when it is completed. He likes Julia's plan for a statue of *Narcissus* lying by the pond, resting on one bent arm, and appearing to look into the water.

He does not believe that *Narcissus* is struck by his own beauty and admiring himself, but rather looking up at the reflection of the sun in the water – the reflection connecting him with Elagabaal, or Heliogabaal, and even imagines that *Narcissus* could be representing Elagabalus himself. Julia was not going to argue. The customer is always right.

Departing, he told them that the guard will bring them to his box at the races because he has many duties he must perform, but after the races the guard can bring them to the palace, where they will be able to relax and meet the other guests.

The palace guard takes them to the Imperial box. The seats have a card with the names of people showing which seats were for them. Julia and Marcus are positioned two rows behind those of Elagabalus' grandmother.

On either side of the grandmother is seated Alexianus, who is Elagabalus young cousin, and the cousin's mother, Mamae on the other side. Showing that the grandmother had plans for her other grandson.

On the other side of the young grandson, Alexianus, sits Comazon. He is the Roman General of *Legio III Gallica* when the family bribed the soldiers into accept Elagabalus as Caracalla's son, and Comazon now serves in the prestigious position as Prefect of the Praetorian Guard.

Comazon, Elagabalus' right-hand man, appears to be supporting the emperor's cousin, rather than being close to the emperor. Elagabalus' position as emperor seems to be weakening and he needs to reassure his grandmother that she has made the right decision, and allow his soldiers to recognise his authority.

Julia notices that one or two senior dignitaries, probably governors of provinces, who are wearing their togas wrapped around them, are sweltering with the heat. Hoping not to be noticed, they have slipped their swollen feet out of their uncomfortable footwear.

On the opposite side of the elongated track Julia searches for Lucy and Petrus, but it is impossible with the thousands of people who have attended.

Lucy is enjoying the new experience of going to the races. Approaching the outer walls of the Circus Maximus she sees small shops selling drinks and food, and various items such as fans, umbrellas, head coverings, and souvenirs. Further along are fortune-tellers trying to predict someone's chances of winning and charging high amounts for their services. On the far outer edges are prostitutes hoping to attract those who have received a lucky win, and have money to spare for a brief awakening.

Before making their entrance into the Circus Maximus, Lucy, Petrus and Sextus buy hot pies, cakes and drinks. It seems that everyone is purchasing food. Lucy places them in a large bag, which she is carrying with her silk shawl inside to cover her head when it the sun is shining.

Leading to the stands are three terraces. To reach these levels are stairways and passages which allow easy access to the seats. The crowd attending could possibly amount to a quarter of a million people all expecting to be seated.

Lucy clings tightly to Petrus, as everyone finds their way to their favourite seating areas. Unlike some other forms of public entertainment, men and women can sit together, and everyone in Rome can attend the Circus Maximus. It is only the senators and dignities that are allowed special seating areas.

Petrus leads the way towards his friends – it is a relief to sit down after being jostled along with the crowd. The seating is narrow and the people are squashed together, practically thigh to thigh. There is plenty of noise and everyone is in great spirits.

People sitting in rows further along from Lucy are pretending that they own horses. They overplay their roles and jokingly call across to each other: 'Hello my good friend. Do you have a horse racing today?' The friend responds, knowing full well that he was not wealthy enough to own a horse. 'Greetings. My best horse running today is named Moly.' The friend replies, 'Is that your horse with black legs and a white body?' 'Yes, so look out for it, because it is beyond your wildest dreams.'

The friends know full well that no such horse is entered in the race, but all those around would spend their time searching for this potential winner.'

They are filling in time, jovially, whilst waiting for the opening procession to begin, and the arrival of dignitaries or the statues of the gods to be honoured, the crowds want to enjoy the entrance of the musicians and the dancers and the excitement of the races.

Some spectators know the names of the horses, others the names of the riders, but everyone has their favourite colours. Red, Blue, Green and White, are the colours shown on the horses and riders, which count more than anything else.

The two women, Lucy and the female friend who Petrus knows, sit next to each other. Petrus' friend sits on the right-hand side of his wife. Petrus sits on the left-hand side of Lucy – their menfolk on the outer side as if protecting them.

Petrus fusses over Lucy, challenging the man who sits behind her and who is massaging his knee up and down Lucy's back. Petrus nudges the man's knee and gives him a rude finger sign.

Lucy moves closer to Petrus, and it gives him the opportunity of putting his arm around her shoulders, as an act of protection. The upper sides of their bodies are in breathing harmony. Lucy occasionally touches his knee, or squeezing his thigh, in excitement. All to his great joy!

Next to Petrus, on his left-hand side, sits Sextus.

On Sextus' left-hand side, positioned next to him, are two ladies in their mid-forties, and after them a man on his own. The two ladies are delighted to find single men on either side. The woman seated next to Sextus flaps her tablet back and forth as if it were a fan, hoping that he notices her.

'I find it is so hot this afternoon, I hope my tablet does not annoy you.'

Sextus knows the woman is trying to flirt with him – this gives him an opportunity to play a flirting game.

'It is very cooling, and I can smell a perfumed wrist as it comes near to me.'

As the conversation progresses between the two women and the two men, they all play a game of secrets and deception.

The women are giving themselves airs-and-graces to trying to show off their clothes, which they purchased the day before, and twirling tablets as fans, and flashing their false eyelashes. But their attire was neither of good quality fabric nor expensive jewellery. It is probably the best the women have ever possessed.

Sextus does not want to say that he has a house in Rome and on the coast, and a wine farm, a theatre, and is a wine merchant. He chooses to pretend to be a manager of an apartment block.

The ladies flirting, say that they would like to visit one of his apartments, perhaps even buy one.

He slightly recognises the other man and hopes that he is not the husband of one of the women, or the boyfriend.

But then remembers that the man has been to a wine tasting at his house, and then recalls that the man is Flavius, the architect. Flavius designed a building on his land where he could store all his wines – a cellar and a small open-air amphitheatre.

He gave Flavius a sly wink. When the woman asked Flavius what he did for a living he said that he ran bread companies. Then realised that he knows nothing about how bread is made. It was all good for laughs, as the woman are not entirely honest.

One said that she is the daughter of Dio Cassius the writer, and the other woman is her sister. The women do not know Dio Cassius but they can see a man in front of them holding a book in his hand with the name and title of a literary work by Dio Cassius. So that is how they now assumed his name as their own.

Sextus is really trying to arrange a date with one of the women. If he can make it happen, then it will be to his pleasure, and impress his doctor that he is not dead yet. He likes to tease his doctor by telling him that he is being kept alive solely on cheap herbs, so that his doctor can enjoy expensive holidays on the fees he charges.

Marcus has no such fun with Julia. They sit as rigid as Elagabalus' grandmother, who wants to show her power over the empire.

Julia notices the first tier of seating facing the large track, is for senators, priests and wealthy equestrians. Elagabalus has probably ignored all protocol to entertain Marcus and Julia, probably wanting to show that he has some authority.

Julia is pleased that they are at the races, with Marcus as her escort.

She touches Marcus on the arm at the beginning of the parade. A long procession of soldiers and dignitaries entered the through the Triumphal Arch which is at the opposite end to the starting point where the charioteers and horses are waiting.

Lucy on her side of the track notices that the race goers seem a bit bored with the parade of the dignitaries. The images of the gods are brought onto the track, by carriage or carriers. The gods are set in place in their usual positions on the racing arena.

The goddess *Magna Mater*, mother earth, known to the Romans as *Cybele*, enters in ceremonial style. Lucy has not seen this goddess before, and notices *Cybele*'s black meteorite stone had been positioned into the statue's face. *Cybele* is paraded around the racetrack on a bier.

But the audience seem more anxious to watch the lively arrival of the men acting as Trojans, and of course the main event, the races.

At last, they stand up with excitement and cheer as the Trojan warriors enter the racetrack. They carry out a war dance representing the Trojan War – Trojans warriors against the Achaean/Greeks warriors. The men have plumed helmets, and their dancing steps involve clashing their shields and knives. Musicians accompany the dancers. The audience love it.

Following this the race goers also enjoy musicians who arrived on the track keeping a musical beat to that of horses' hooves as they galloped around at a musical trot.

Satyrs are now ready for their performance. The crowd go wild with excitement. Men appear wearing clothing to imitate satyrs, with long ears and tails and each with a very long penis. They perform lewd dancing, whilst garlands of flowers around their necks sway back and forth to the rhythm. The public are accustomed to the performance of satyrs as they are often seen dancing at funerals, but not as spectacular when appearing with such a large group of performers.

There is a short pause and Petrus explains to Lucy that, 'the racetrack is approximately six hundred paces in length. The horses are to come through the gates and run counter-clockwise, around a dividing central area of the track returning to where they began and then repeat the process.

The dividing central area, which is about four paces wide, is called the spina. The horses run seven laps around the spina.

At the end of the spina, Lucy noticed that there are large eggs. Petrus explains that in earlier times they used figures of dolphins, representing the god *Neptune*, as counters, so that the spectators can see how many laps have been covered. These were changed to eggs, and after each lap an egg is removed.

He tells Lucy – 'When you see the charioteers making their horses go close to the turning end they place themselves in danger. Charioteers could receive the blow of a whip from an opponent, supposedly intended for hitting his own or his opponents' horses, which is severe if it catches eyes or face. Or a whip can become entangled in a horse's reigns, legs or tail, or the legs or arms of a charioteer. The bit in the horse's mouth could be pulled severely by a charioteer trying to make the turn, cutting into the horse's tongue.'

'Charioteers place the whip in their right hand and the reigns of each horse in their left, and wrapping the reigns around his chest to steer using his body and legs. You will notice, that the charioteers wear a torso support with lacing to tie the bodice tight. Held in this is a curved knife, which is used to cut a charioteer free if there is danger of an accident, especially the prospect of being dragged under chariot wheels or horses' hooves. He also wears leather straps on his legs for protection.'

Lucy becomes more interested, especially when Petrus said that she can choose the colour of a team and he will place a bet for her. She chose the blue team.

He tells her, 'Of course if a charioteer is racing for the reds and the emperor likes the green team, then perhaps he could be in a difficult situation if the red team beat that of the emperor's choice.'

Lucy looks toward the twelve starting gates, but she was too far away to identify any of the horses, just the colour of the charioteer was what she looks for – but unfortunately her colour lost that race.

Between the races there are musicians and dancers to hold people's attention. It gives everyone time for refreshments and talk.

She enjoys watching riders when they leap between two yoked horses, or seeing charioteers running alongside their chariots, which is particularly dangerous.

Sextus, turns to Petrus and Lucy, saying that he had not been to the races for some time.

'On that particular occasion, I had attended the races at the Campus Martius, not far from the Circus Maximus, but just further north. It was October and I was excited that the two horses running the race, much to my excitement, won.'

'Then, at the end of the two-horse race, I found to my horror that the winning horse positioned on the inside, would have to have its tail cut off and then its head also cut off as was the custom. After that I could not face going to the races until now.'

'Just as well that it's not October – thank goodness,' says Lucy.

*

There is an accident at the Circus Maximus and the crowds are making 'ooo' and aah' sounds. Some say that a charioteer has fallen and been hurt.

On Julia and Marcus' side of the track they can see that the young man has removed his helmet. The race is temporarily stopped, whilst the organisers carry him off the track.

Throughout the disturbance Marcus notices some officials speaking quietly to Elagabalus. The emperor moves out of the stadium.

After a short time Elagabalus' relatives all leave.

The Praetorian Guard, who earlier escorted Marcus and Lucy, asks them to come with him. He leads them away from the area.

'You may have noticed when the charioteer fell, he stood up, he removed his helmet. It was at that moment Elagabalus noticed how handsome he was with his blonde hair falling from his helmet. One of Elagabalus' personal helpers went to the charioteer and said that the emperor wishes him to come to the palace.'

'News has come back that the emperor has told his servants to prepare his bath with perfume and flowers so that he may bathe with the charioteer.

'The racing will continue, as this is what the crowds expect, but Elagabalus' grandmother and the rest in this box have left the races. There will be no gathering at the palace, which Elagabalus invited you to, after the race, because he wishes to privately entertain the young charioteer.'

Marcus turns to the guard. 'Thank you for the information, I shall tell Julia.'

'I understand that the charioteer's name is Hierocles. Has a great manly physique that made him most appealing to Elagabalus,' says the guard.

Some weeks later Marcus hears stories that Elagabalus is infatuated with "his blonde husband" and enjoys being beaten by him, often receiving a black eye – making Elagabalus love his husband even more.

Hierocles firmly positions himself within the emperor's inner circle, causing the emperor's own position to be in danger, yet he ignores hints made by the guards to remove Hierocles.

The soldiers grow to disrespect their emperor's weakness. They desire a stronger man who can lead them into battle such an occasion arise.

CHAPTER SIX

Travelling to Capri and Tales of Corinth

When Julia and Lucy arrive at the Tiber River dockside, Marcus and Petrus had already organised the loading of the *Victory* statue onto a moored boat.

It is the first time that the women have been to this dock and it seems quite chaotic to them, but after noticing the name of their boat and the mooring they ignore the distractions of the other vessels being loaded nearby.

Making their way to the boat, they notice a beggar with a small miserable monkey dressed in red clothing, banging a tiny drum with a stick and it turns around as if dancing. When tiredness overcomes the animal, the owner hits it with a small whip. The animal has no teeth. Next to it is a small tired dog, performing summersaults – both animals have chains around their necks. Julia and Lucy give each animal a small piece of food.

A little further along is a beggar with his palms extended. He is seeking money for his children. He has a drawing of three stick figures on a piece of board, which is supposed to represent his children of different age groups.

Julia and Lucy notice the children nearby, who are very thin and poorly clothed. Not all the poor were on the state list to receive free bread and oil. Julia gives the father three coins – hoping that the money will go towards the children and not to toast the god of wine.

Gundher helps Lucy and Julia onto the gangplank and organises their luggage on board. He had earlier been helping Marcus and Petrus with the statues. Gundher then leaves to return to the showroom.

The boat is flat-bottomed and the statue is positioned at the furthest end from Julia and Lucy. Two oxen begin to tow the barge slowly towards Ostia, a main port on the coast. Julia decides to curl up and sleep. Lucy is far more anxious – she wonders if she can swim to the side of the bank should the boat sink. Then she becomes distracted, noticing several small boats busily taking their trade up and down the Tiber.

There were larger boats, such as the *caudicariae* (long boats) transporting large quantities of corn up the river from Ostia. The speed of the vessels being dependent upon the river tides as well as the oxen.

Africans, Greeks, Egyptians and people from various other countries are all working on or around the Tiber and ports, manoeuvring vessels up and down.

Lucy tries to imagine how difficult it must have been when the huge and heavy obelisk, some years earlier, had been brought from Egypt, and then placed on barges up the Tiber River to Rome.

Eventually Julia, Marcus, Lucy and Petrus reached the port of Ostia, on the Tyrrhenian Sea.

Marcus leaves them exploring the docks, whilst he goes further along the quay to the *horrea*, or warehouses, some of these being multi-storeyed. The manager, an employee at Sextus' warehouse, has organised their travel arrangements to Capri, and the return journey by road. Two warehouse workers will be accompanying them, who previously had been sailors, but left their shipping companies to live closer to home and work at the warehouse and dockside.

They will take care of the statue and the two busts, as well as prepare drinks and a little food at the small galley kitchen on board the ship, and assist Marcus on the return journey.

Whilst Marcus is organising their voyage, Petrus takes the women for a walk around the port. They realise how lucky they are having the warehouse manager, and Marcus being a friend of the ship's owner, and the shipping agent to sort out all their needs.

Other travellers upon arrival at Ostia need to find shipping agents to supply them with information about sailing times, shipping destinations and booking arrangements. This can be arduous if passengers, accompanied by their many slaves, all need tickets and space before making their way up the gangplank.

Petrus, Julia and Lucy, walk along the walled quayside where there are cranes and men moving heavy cargo. Some containers are being uploaded onto ships, ready to depart, whilst other ships arrive at the port, with their cargo from various countries.

Listed on the outside of the arriving crates, are names of various products, such as marble, silk fabrics, dyes, spices, timber, from China, India, France, North Africa. Some could have come partly overland before reaching the Mediterranean Sea.

On the dockside they notice a crane lowering sponges secured in a large net. These are to be loaded into a smaller boat to go up the Tiber River.

Slave workers will be employed to attach sticks or handles to the sponges, so that these each become cleaning items for lavatory use. Many Romans used slaves to clean their bottoms with these sponge sticks.

Petrus tells Lucy the well-known story of a gladiator who did not want to go into the arena and fight, and stuck one of these sponge sticks down his throat to choke himself to death.

Ships entering the harbour are liable for tax or port usage, and importers of goods paying customs duty. Julia notices a man checking the ship's manifest for clearance purposes.

The favourable time of the year for sailing is between early spring and late summer, which is when most ships sailing on the Mediterranean receive favourable winds. During the winter months, most ships are kept in various ports or safe harbours.

Julia, Lucy and Petrus, are not ready to board their merchant ship, but can see its name on either side of the stern – it is called *Apollo*. They stroll further along the quayside, passing by taverns, food sellers and shops which display scarves, broaches, and ornamental carved ships.

Several tourists and sailors are purchasing wooden carvings of the god *Priapus* who is depicted with an extremely large penis. Petrus quietly explains to Lucy that *Priapus* is a rustic god and the son of *Dionysus*. He is a god who protects crops and is placed in agricultural fields by farmers hoping for a good harvest.

The people who want to purchase the carving of the god, have no intention of placing the artefact in their fields, but wish to buy it for themselves or friends because it has such a monstrous appendage, and it provides them with good humour.

'Do you want one Lucy,' asked Julia jokingly.

'Certainly not! But why is *Priapus* so ugly?'

'From what I understand of the story, the goddess *Hera*, being the wife of *Zeus*, had caused *Priapus* to become grotesque and to possess a large permanent erection, but at the same time making him impotent. It was his punishment for saying that *Aphrodite* was more beautiful than *Hera*.'

'He is often reddish in colour, and seen as a god from Hellespont wearing Phrygian cap and boots.'

As they move away from the tourist shop they see a large carved figure of *Priapus* with a notice saying, "I was once a discarded trunk of a tree and with the skill of a wood carver, using his best tool and red polish, I became the image of the god *Priapus*".

Lucy refers back to the comment about why *Priapus* was punished. 'I don't remember ever hearing about the goddess *Hera* wanting to be more beautiful than *Aphrodite*,' said Lucy.

'Well you will learn more about the goddess *Hera* when my father has his birthday party, which he holds every second year, and he is having one this year,' said Julia.

'I am going to persuade him to invite all of my friends to the party. He normally invites his friends and senators for a weekend game to re-enact the ancient Trojan War between Achaean/Greeks and Trojans. During this time one hears so many of the names of the gods, and then you will understand more about *Hera* and *Aphrodite.*

Further along the dockside are beggars – one has a dirty old bandage wrapped around his hand. On a piece of board in front of him is written: "I was shipwrecked – please help my family". They give him a small amount of money.

Men did get injured at sea – many ships sank when overloaded and in poor weather conditions. A sailor, with injuries was no good for working on ships at sea, nor at the dockside. They are left to become forgotten men.

They meet up again with Marcus and make their way to the '*Apollo*'.

Their ship has three decks. He tells them about the ship. 'It is on its way to Syria, but the captain is making a special route. The ship plans to make a stop at Sorrento but before reaching the port he will go close to the isle Capri so that we can disembark and travel by a smaller boat. Depending upon the weather conditions.'

They tour the decks to see where the statue will be placed. Then explore the upper deck, and the poop deck and where the helmsman is positioned.

After seeing a little of the ship, and feeling lost between the crowds and the crew, they are taken to meet the Captain. There is a small cabin for Lucy and Julia to share. Marcus and Petrus are shown their sleeping quarters with bunk beds.

The ship is made ready to leave the quay and go out beyond the harbour wall. Sailors in unison pull up the topsail, the square shaped mainsail that is in the middle, and foresail. Before long they are out in the Tyrrhenian Sea.

With good sailing conditions they should reach their destination the following evening or the morning after – it all depends upon having good winds. Lucy does not like the thought of being at sea for too long.

When further out to sea, Lucy faces the wind and stands holding onto the side of the ship on one of the lower decks. She looks over at the fishes swimming alongside the side of the ship. Petrus joins her and they stand close together.

Neither hear the crew's orders being given when the sailors adjust the sails to catch the wind. The new course brings the wind in a different direction, causing Lucy's shawl to loosen and wrap itself around both Lucy and Petrus.

The crew noticed this it causes them laughter and make comments that they looked like twin Egyptian mummies.

The two dockworkers from the warehouse who are in charge of the statue, have found a safe spot where they can sleep close by the statue. They have taken with them a supply of oil, water, and sufficient food for the journey, and a small amphora of wine. At nightfall they light an oil lamp to play dice or a board game, each having a small container to hold pomegranate seeds, which they use a pinch to bet against each other.

Next morning Lucy is feeling sick. The sea becomes choppy. One person tells her to make for the centre of the ship – another to lie down – another to go to the top rear deck.

Everyone worries – because if she is sick over the side, nobody wants her to be facing the wind when this happens.

A sailor seeing how pale Lucy had become, brings her some hard sea biscuits to nibble on, and tells her to lie down in the cabin.

By the afternoon the winds had calmed, and the sun is shining. Lucy joins the others on the deck.

The *Victory* statue had been tied to a post but after the severe wind some of the wrapping and ties had loosened. Petrus, with the two dockworkers, go to secure the wrapping, and make the statue more secure again.

The men give Petrus a few seeds to nibble whilst he is working, but he leaves them in the dish to one side until he finishes the work.

One worker holds the lower part of the statue in place – the other worker at the back of the statue is securing it with ropes.

Petrus is left to hold the body of the statue upright. He places his hands on each smooth marble breast of the *Victory* statue, to stop it from leaning forward. After securing the statue Petrus eats a few seeds, but throws a few into the sea because they have little pieces of hard pomegranate skin.

Upon returning to the statue, he notices a few sailors in a line coming up to the statue and placing both hands on each breast. Then taking a pinch of the pomegranate pips, eating one or two, and tipping the rest of the seeds left in their hand into the sea.

As the walk away, two more sailors do the same thing. Hands on each breast and so on.

'Please don't stop them – they think that you have been making an offering to the goddess for a safe journey,' the captain tells Petrus.

'But the statue is supposed to be going to the ship's owner, and the white marble will have black greasy finger marks on the breasts.'

'They will think it's a bad omen if they can't continue ... then they won't work until there is a sign or a good omen.'

'I will speak to the dockworkers and tell them that it looks like their pomegranate pips will have to be shared with the crew of the ship,' says Marcus.

The ritual carries on until they reach their destination.

Marcus seeing Petrus holding the breasts of the goddess and asks Petrus what he experienced. 'Feeling the statue felt - erm – I can't quite think of the word I'm looking for ...'

'What about uplifting, arousing, restful?'

'Floating – I think that's the word.'

'You are right about the floating feeling – remember we are on a ship at sea,' comments Marcus.

'Well, perhaps a moment of bliss.' Hoping that his reply will make Marcus happy – he just felt that he was holding in place a piece of marble, which felt cool at the touch.

The weather has improved and the captain decides to take the ship as close as possible to the isle of Capri, where smaller boats come alongside.

Julia and Lucy are the first ones to be taken to Capri. Slowly the statues and busts are lowered into other boats.

The crew are sorry to see the statue of *Victory* leave the ship but Marcus informs them that the owner of the ship shall be placing the statue outside his house on the Isle of Capri, looking out to the Tyrrhenian Sea. So perhaps they may see the statue, but if not, they know that it is there, looking outwards to the sea.

Capri has a small pier and dockside where there are donkeys to carry the goods up the hillside – some have baskets affixed on either side, others have seating on their backs, and some pull carts.

Whilst the men are all busy off-loading the goods onto the island, Julia and Lucy decide to take a leisurely walk to the top towards the house. They are pleased to just walk upon firm ground, after the movement on board the ship at sea.

They notice that the sea close to the island is a turquoise-blue and very clear, turning to clear emerald green in places near the rocky inlets.

A man leading the donkey places their luggage in baskets attached to either side of the animal and walks on ahead.

Also accompanying them is a guide who occasionally points out places of interest, such as where emperor Tiberius had built several villas on the island around two hundred years earlier. "Villa Jovis" the main palace for the emperor, was several thousand square metres in size. It was built on a promontory of steep land that required stairways to connect each level built into hillside.

As they travel further up the gravel path, there are direction posts made of wood. Each post is carved with the head of the god *Hermes*, the god of travellers. The guide tells them that such posts are called Herms or Hermae. They are made of stone or wood – with a carved head and shoulders and then the vertical post is positioned into the ground. Some even had small testicles, an indication that it was representing the god guiding the way. These are Greek boundary markers. The Romans have markers named after the god *Terminus* defining boundaries, whereas the god *Hermes* also shows the way.

Some people also used a small pile of stones – others used just pieces of wood. But it shows that

Captain Lycus cares for historical sculptures by Romans or Greeks, no matter how small the item.

Just as they reach the top of the hill where the Captain's house stands is a carved marble statue of *Hermes*. The god is wearing a travellers' cloak, a *chlamys*, and a round hat decorated with wings on either side. In his left hand is a *caduceus* or long stick with two twisted snakes and eagle wings on the very top.

'At last *Hermes* has brought us safely to the house,' says Lucy and leaves the god a small flower of appreciation.

They can see the captain approaching. His eyes scan all the furniture and cushions as he walks across the garden, past the swimming pool with chairs scattered, on his way to greet them. He has not lost the touch of 'Captain's inspection' even though semi-retired. Somehow his head gardener notices one of his boss's authoritarian flash looks, and immediately rushes to pick up leaves that have blown into the edge of the pool.

Greeting them, he shows them the grounds, the house, and then the guesthouse where they will sleep. Drinks are placed in their rooms and he asks them to join him on the terrace after they have rested.

The workers manage to slowly bring, up to the front of the house, the *Victory* statue and unwrap all its protective covering. The wall length doors and windows are wide open and the statue is temporarily placed in front facing the sea, but needs repairs to secure the base – so they provide stones to hold it in place.

Lycus examines the damage that happened in the library gardens in Rome. He says that a skilled sculptor in Sorrento, a friendly Greek like himself, will be able to make good repairs.

Petrus explains the breast touching story. Lycus decides that it adds to its history. He tells Lycus, 'the smooth texture of the marble was cool to touch.'

Lycus decides that he will place is hands on the goddess' breast and said that all his visitors are going to feel in a good state of mind.

When Lucy and Julia eventually change and come out onto the terrace to join the others, Lycus is already seated by the swimming pool, accompanied by a very bronze and glamorous woman in her early twenties.

Turning to them she says, 'The captain calls me 'Honey-bee – my real name is 'mmmmm' – she murmurs but please all call me 'Honey-bee'. All the men practically 'purr' with approval. Lucy and Julia have no intention of calling her anything like that but decide to mumble the first bit 'mmmmm … hello, lovely to meet you.'

Lycus explains how he first met Honey-Bee. 'I was working at that time as ship's captain and had a few days spare when the ship was at Corinth. My very distant relatives were from Corinth, so I took with me "A Guide to Greece" written by Pausanias, and travelled as a tourist in search of the city's history and ancient monuments.'

Unfortunately, around four hundred years ago, a certain Roman named Mummius had used Corinth as his threat to the rest of Greece, or Achaea, to submit to becoming part of Roman provinces, otherwise they would face the same consequences as Corinth which he destroyed. He killed all the men. Woman and children were sold as slaves.'

'It is said that he had no interest in the culture of Corinth, or its art history, or its artefacts. Yet, strangely for a man of little artistic taste, he removed all these valuable items to be sent to Rome, before raising the city to the ground.'

'So you can understand my appreciation to Pausanius who, a few hundred years later, wrote his travel book, allowing me to enjoy the spirit of Corinth,' said Lycus.

'When I returned to the ship a beautiful woman stood before me. "My world has collapsed", she said, and on the verge of tears.

'I wondered to myself what dreadful thing could have happened.

'I would like to help, please tell me your problem?'

'My fingernail has broken, and I do not have any scissors.

'I thought to myself, perhaps life is too short to take on the worries of everything. She sat down beside me, whilst I became her hero of the moment, and trimmed her nail.

'Then she told me her story.

'She was to travel from Athens to Corinth to marry a second cousin, and meet her future husband's family there, and then after the marriage ceremony, both were to travel on to Sicily. But on meeting her at Corinth he told that her loved another woman. Rather than return to her home, she decided to continue the voyage to Sicily, feeling too sad to face her family and friends.'

Lycus places his hand on Honey-Bee and continues with the story. 'I told her that I would see that she gets to Sicily. But if she likes my idea, she could go to my house in Capri where I have a local couple looking after my house and a young man who looks after the grounds. But she could work for me making the house look comfortable and homely, and the garden more creative with all my statues and plants. After a very short time we married.

'From then onwards I decided to name her Honey-Bee, instead of Melissa.'

Whilst Lycus had been telling his story, everyone then glanced towards her – lying on a sunbed nearby having her toenails painted by a slave and with a rather small robe wrapped around her body as she applied oil to her arms and shoulders.

All the men's eyes were on each slow stroke, as she lay back. Her robe gently resting above her knees, and one leg spread onto cushions. She appears to like being noticed. She gave little shrieks and giggles saying, 'Oh that tickles' - as a drop of oil trickles down her arm and onto her thigh.'

The friends slowly grow accustomed to hearing the name Honey-Bee, and found themselves also naming her by that name.

Julia asks what she does in the garden. 'I spent my time on Capri going from plant to plant on the hillside, checking on their local names, and take cuttings. My dried flower arrangements are sold at the local shops to tourists.

Men listened to her every word. It was not what she said, but she mesmerised them with the slowly pursing of her lips and bashfully raising her eyes at the same time catching each of the man's eyes in turn, so each felt individually connected with her. Her hands, body and tanned legs move in a slow sensual way – occasionally swishing her blonde hair away in slow movement.

'I collect anything I can find on the shoreline, and create small decorative designs for the tourists to take back a souvenir for their friends. I also take tourists around the island and show them Lycus' collection of statues which mainly relate to the sea.'

Honey-bee walks indoors to put on some sandals, and asks Julia and Lucy to accompany her down to the beach.

The men take a stroll around the top of the island, with Lycus explaining places of interest.

Residents on the island pay for sentries to guard the dockside entrance to prevent unwelcomed visitors,' says Lycus.

'There are now many residents taking an interest in maintaining their gardens amongst the rugged and jagged rocks – all providing various pleasant resting areas for those wishing to sit and enjoy the sea view.'

They wander around Capri, noticing peregrine falcons flying overhead, pine trees with blackbirds resting on branches, geckos lazing against the warm rocks and one or two blue lizards. They continue their walk down to the cave – the Blue Grotto - and gaze at the clear blue-green colour of the water.

'Why did you choose to live here?' asks Marcus.

'Well I am of Greek descent, and often sail to Athens and one or two islands, and Capri reminds me of the islands of Greece and its people. The night sky is very clear and the view is fantastic.'

'Have you heard the expression *Halcyon* days?' Nobody replies.

'Well, according to an old myth it refers to fourteen days in the winter when storms never occur.

'*Halcyon*, a goddess, did not want her husband *Ceyx* going to sea during winter months – but he left, because he wished to go to the oracle to seek advice.

'She was right to have concern. Her beloved *Ceyx* lost his life during the journey when there was terrible storm.

'Distraught, when *Halcyon* saw her husband's body washed up on the shore, *Morpheus*, the god of dreams, disguised himself as *Ceyx*.

'Seeing her husband's apparition, *Halcyon* threw her body into the sea to join him.

'The gods, showing such compassion, and in order to keep alive the name *Halcyon* – they changed them both into birds.

'*Halcyon* and *Ceyx* became kingfishers. In order that she may lay her eggs and nest on the rocky shore, her father, *Aeolus*, son of *Poseidon*, the god of winds – calms the seas, and eases the winds.

'Seas and winds ease for seven days on each side of the shortest day of the year.'

Lycus stops them from walking further along the path.

'One of the marble statue heads or busts which you brought with you was of *Aeolus*, and not

Poseidon. I shall place it at this spot where you are now standing.'

'It is far more interesting now that you have told us this story,' says Petrus.

'These are my – *Halcyon* days' – said Lycus – 'days of peace and calm.'

Lycus leaves the men wandering around and returns to the house.

Marcus and Petrus wonder what had happened to the girls, and peer down from the high cliffs.

The sun is slowly setting and they can see the women on the beach laughing and leaping in and out of the sea. Then they stand looking out to sea and Marcus and Petrus can see the light shining through their damp clothing. They both wished that they could be down on the beach as well, but they do not want to appear as if they were spying from the top of Capri.

After an evening meal by the pool they sit and talk of Greece and Italy.

Sadly, the day came when it was time to leave Capri. The captain, upon receiving the carvings, gives Lucy plenty of money, enough to cover expenses and profit and to generously pay Papinus.

Slaves help them down the hillside to the small boats, and across to Sorrento. Not on the bay side, which had slightly suffered when Vesuvius erupted and the ashes covered Herculaneum and Pompey some years earlier, but on the southern side – where men still sail their boats and have farm-fishing areas.

It is time to travel by boat up the west coast, northward towards Baiae. It was, and still is, a great retirement and holiday area known for its warm sulphur springs. Romans and Greeks also make a living carving sculptures of the goddess *Venus*, or *Aphrodite* her Greek name. One hundred years earlier the emperor Hadrian died at his dwelling at Baiae.

After Baiae their journey continues on land to Terracina, where the Senator's friends were expecting them to spend the night.

CHAPTER SEVEN

Venus One and Cheaper Venus Two

Gundher hears through the grapevine that Crispus has gone away to visit his father, so decides that it is time to swop the statue in his front garden.

The statue is being held in the store at the back of the showroom premises. If Crispus does not pay the bill for the expensive statue, then after some period of time they may sell the expensive one in order to recover some of the losses that will occur. Should he eventually pay his bill, they can reverse the procedure and return the original statue and remove the cheaper version.

The senator's elderly gardener, who rarely speaks, and seems to forget what he is doing, has been told by Gundher and Ndio that he must bring the cart to the showroom.

They decide that sunset shall be the best time. Nobody is going to notice another mule-pulled cart on the road.

The gardener and Gundher wrap the cheaper version in sacking. Gundher sits in the back of the cart supporting the statue, and dressed as a lowly workman, whilst Ndio sits beside the gardener in the front, having applied make-up to appear as his elderly wife. At least they do not need to ask the gardener to keep quiet and not make a sound.

They park outside Crispus' house. Ndio and Gundher go into the garden and begin, slowly and carefully to remove the stone and rubble supporting the statue, then to carry it to the wagon. It is quite heavy, but he is a tall strong man.

They can hear the nailed boots of the city guards walking along the street, and hope that they will not go near the donkey cart and gardener.

Soon the sounds of the footsteps disappear.

Ndio and Gundher carry the cheaper version to the garden.

They just hope that there is nobody around, because it looks like they are taking bodies of young, semi-naked women back and forth.

When the cheaper statue is in place in the garden, they manage to tidy up the area, and just hope that that anyone looking at it in the morning would just think that a dog had unsettled the soil.

Ndio and Gundher are now in the wagon. Ndio is in the front next to the old gardener. Gundher lies in the back carefully supporting the expensive statue next to his body, like a pair of lovers. He knows the craftsman who made the sculpture and does not wish to see one part of it chipped or broken.

They are all tired and decide to rest for a few minutes before returning to the showroom – Gundher says that he would keep watch.

Gundher did not watch too hard and keeps closing his eyes – part awake and part asleep.

He hears a loud clang and looks towards Crispus' garden to see a woman trying to smash the new, and fortunately cheaper statue he has just placed in the garden.

He dashes up and finds her somewhat drunk. After taking away her wooden weapon, which turns out to be a broken tree branch, Gundher calms her down. She tells him about her life with Crispus' father who has now died, and how she has been thrown out of the house by the farm manager, and she wonders why Crispus has done this to her.

She begins wailing. 'How am I to find somewhere to live and sleep – nobody cares about me.'

Gundher calms her down and gives her some money to spend the night in a tavern, and tells her to return to the farm and speak with the farm manager.

Ndio had earlier told Gundher that Crispus had gone to see his father. All the gossip came to her in the showroom. So Gundher suggests that she should return to the farm and speak with the farm manager and Crispus.

He watches her depart, no doubt to spend the money drinking the night away.

After she departs, Gundher, Ndio and the gardener have to remove the damaged statue. Smooth out the ground around it, and place the good and expensive statue back in its place.

The broken and cheaper statue is now with them in the cart. Gundher can see that it is slightly damaged but it is still possible to repair and sell it.

All in all, it has been a very exhausting and not a successful evening.

They are now ready to return and pleased to be on their way as the evening is becoming quite chilly.

The cold night air is having an effect on the old gardener. He says that he needs to relieve himself, and finds a tree in the garden that suits his purpose, close to the statue. He is standing reasonably erect and ready to perform, when a man and his wife, who seem to be neighbours of Crispus, walk down the road. The gardener stands erect, fixing his eyes on the trunk of the tree.

The neighbour comments as he walks past. 'I do wish Crispus would stop putting statues in his front garden.' They look at the old gardener. 'This one of *Priapus* is definitely letting the neighbourhood down!'

But as soon as they continue down the road, the old gardener finishes urinating in the garden – unfortunately, having undergone under such stress, he forgets where he is, and starts to take off the dead heads of the flowers in Crispus' garden.

Ndio takes his arm and brings him back to the wagon and they return somewhat disappointed.

*

A few days later, Crispus' maid is in the showroom chatting with Ndio about the gossip she had heard about Elagabalus. Her days are devoted to the

Madam and the house, and providing the maid with little contact of the world outside the household.

Everyone in Rome knows that Elagabalus loves Hierocles, his charioteer, but the latest gossip that the maid reveals to Ndio is that the emperor has been presented by his friends with another young man – an athlete, a very able young man. A physically endowed man, named Zoticus, who is appoint to the position as the emperor's chamberlain.

'I have heard that Zoticus has a beautiful athletic body, but his private parts, are greater than what most men possess,' said the maid.

'Upon meeting the emperor, Zoticus addresses him as "Hail, my Lord Emperor" and the response from Elagabalus was not what Zoticus expected. He chose to act in a coy feminine manner, pointing out to him "I am a Lady" replied the emperor.

"Zoticus, is the new love of the emperor's life.

'However, Hierocles, is not happy to just lie back. He does not want Zoticus to become firmly rooted within the palace. He decides to make a plan to make the emperor dissatisfied with the athlete.

'Cupbearers loyal to Hierocles give the newcomer a drug to make Zoticus impotent.

'Zoticus had a night of complete erection malfunction.

'Unable to satisfy Elagabalus' needs he was unceremoniously driven from not only the palace but also from Rome.'

Ndio was undecided whether to inform the senator about this latest news about Zoticus, Hierocles and the emperor – but then decides that he probably knows all about the short adventurous life of Zoticus.

*

After sailing up the coast from Sorrento to Baiae, Marcus and Petrus are fighting off tiredness. They continue their journey by covered wagon, a *carpentum,* which has four wheels. Julia is asleep and Marcus manages to squeeze himself on the end of her seat.

Lucy tries to close her eyes to relieve the boredom and monotony. Suddenly, the carriage is slowly brought to a halt.

Darkness is drawing in and the two men go outside to speak with the driver to ask why the wagon has stopped.

'One of the horses has slightly injured its right leg, and needs to be taken for veterinary treatment in the next town which is about seven miles away. I will take the horse and exchange if for another,' says the driver.

'I will send one of my men with you. We will wait here in the carriage,' replies Marcus.

He instructed one of the dockworkers. 'Go with the driver and the horse, see that the driver changes horses and returns straight away. I do not want him drinking in the tavern all night. Here is some money to pay for all the expenses and, when you return, bring some food and drink for the rest of the journey.'

The horse and driver, accompanied by the warehouse man from the docks, make their way slowly up the road with the horse slightly limping.

Marcus is watching them disappear into the distance, and the moonlit sky, when Petrus and Lucy join him.'

'Lucy and I have decided to walk to the house where the senator's friend lives, so that Lucy get a good night's sleep. Perhaps you will be joining us quite soon.'

Marcus gives Petrus them directions and the name of the family who are to be their hosts.

Petrus and Lucy disappear up the hill, with their limited information. Petrus begins to search for milestones along the way as reference points, as well as looking for the North Star.

The remaining dockworker is sitting in the front of the vehicle keeping his eyes on the road ahead. It is not safe to sit around on deserted roads at nightfall because there is a chance of being robbed.

Marcus returns to the wagon and closes his eyes.

Later in the evening twilight, the dockworker notices three men standing on the side of the road much further away. They have been stopping passers-by and harassing them for money or goods.

Julia is fast asleep, when the dockworker taps Marcus on the shoulder and signals him to join him outside.

'You should be careful about those men in the distance, because they are robbers and it looks like they are slowly making their way down the road – possibly wondering why this vehicle is not moving and whether it has been abandoned.

'They will notice your shoes and madam's jewellery and good quality garments that she is wearing – you can be robbed by these ruffians.

'Perhaps you should get the madam to change her clothes because she looks wealthy. Then make your way up the hill to the house of your friends before she faces any danger.'

Marcus does not want the dockworker in danger, nor have the man run away. 'Take this money, because they will expect something, and we do not want all our possessions stolen.'

Marcus wonders how long it would take to wake up Julia. To argue with her will cause delays, as she will want to discuss all the options of leaving or staying. On second thoughts, it was better to just take action and argue about it later.

He decides that the best idea is to make her look poor. If the thieves come close and see Julia as a poor old lady, with nothing of value, she will probably be left alone.

In her present state, she looks wealthy with her jewelled broach, expensive embroidery edges on her clothing, her make-up and hair with jewelled combs.

Due to the travelling, Julia is in a deep sleep. He has no time to talk and discuss matters with her.

Quickly he finds some of Julia's silk shawls in her luggage. He removes some of her outer clothing to turn it inside-out, so that no braided embroidery is showing on the edges of her clothing. She was now in her underwear consisting of a band to cover her breasts and a small V-shaped material band being her underwear.

Instead of making her look like an old lady, he decides to make her look poor and pregnant. Her small band of underwear can hold a scarf in place against her stomach. He places one to hold the shawl against her stomach and uses another to tie it in place.

Feeling pleased with his ingenuity and quick thinking, he begins to do a little humming whilst he works.

Julia wakes up. She begins to hit at his rump that is positioned towards her face. He turns around quickly finished then places his hand over her mouth.

'It's all for your own protection – robbers are coming closer.'

He raids her bag with one hand – the other on her mouth indicating that she must remain quiet. He roughs up her hair, removes any jewellery, raids her cosmetics, and mascara to make her eyes and face look poor and grey. Marcus also makes himself look like a poor man.

The dockworker sitting at the front of the vehicle can barely recognise them.

'I will take the madam just up the hill and leave her in a safe place and come back and help you if there is any trouble.'

'No need to come back, just stay with the madam to get her safely away,' he replies.

Before leaving the dock worker he gives him some money to pacify the robbers.

Marcus lifts Julia onto his shoulder and rushes up the hill and lowers her to the ground when they are out of sight.

By the time Marcus looks back through the shrubbery at the carriage the robbers have approached the worker. They seem to be talking. Then the worker gives them some money, which seems to make them satisfied and they continue down the road.

After climbing and walking over boundary walls and small rocks, Marcus loses his grip on a branch and slips. He sprains his ankle. They now look dishevelled and in need of bathing, nourishment and sleep. He finds a long stick to help support his walking.

Eventually they reach a stream and manage to clean themselves and take a rest. Marcus chooses this moment to tell the whole story of Sextus, and his promise to keep the secret of being in disguise, as requested by Sextus. He also tells her about his idea for her business.

'You can export smaller sculptures, items for people's gardens, paintings of flowers, landscapes, and fruit and fish – or whatever people like, and of course beautiful Italian glassware and tableware.'

She is quite keen on the idea of improving her business.

They are so wrapped up with enthusiasm for the future that they forget about the removal of the clothing to make Julia look pregnant.

Eventually they arrive at the house of the senator's friends.

After telling them about their travels to and from Capri, the owners said that they had been waiting for them to arrive and food has been prepared.

'We did not know that you are pregnant. How delightful – we will let you eat early and have a night's sleep because you are probably exhausted.'

The hosts explain that they have moved to a small house and are going to live in Baiae. But after receiving a note about Julia's arrival they have kept a bed, but they have little furniture. Everything else is at our house down on the coast.'

Julia feels that this was not the moment to discuss why her stomach was padded out, because the hosts were too sincere and had gone out of their way to offer their limited hospitality.

They are offered soup. 'Would you like thick or thin soup,' asks the hostess. They are both hungry and say that they would like thick.

The soup arrives looking like coloured hot water with three small beans and a tiny part of a turnip. They wonder what the thin soup looks like. The next course has a spray of parsley covering an S-shaped brown fish, full of bones, and a small spoonful of *garum,* fish sauce.

The hosts go out to the kitchen and Marcus looks through the window to see if he can see Petrus and Lucy. He notices that a dog outside the house has a huge bowl of goat meat and Marcus was considering whether the dog is treated better than the guests.

Just then the hosts returns with the next course. The main course was blackish rough grained bread, a display of tiny sparrows enough for about two each, and some local garden vegetables. But there were plenty of small biscuits.

Julia ponders whether the hosts normally eat this sort of food, or had it been a special meal for their visit. It was an acquired taste. But then Julia notices their thin bodies and wonders whether they are very short of money.

They notice Marcus looking at the dog.

'That is our lovely dog called Dromas. We named him after one of the dogs in Ovid's "Metamorphoses" story about Acteon's dogs that were all given names. We chose Dromas, because it means runner, and he loves to chase rabbits. Unfortunately, we can't take him with us down to the coast, so our neighbour has agreed to keep him and feeds him. But he still loves to be around the house.

After the meal, Marcus says that he must have a quick search to find out what has happened to Petrus and Lucy.

*

There are only a few farmhouses in the area, not particularly close to each other. Some have no lights on.

At the third farmhouse lamps are burning, and through a window he sees Petrus and Lucy eating. He knocks on the door.

They tell Marcus the story of their arrival at the farmstead, which they thought was the house belonging to the senator's hosts.

They tell Marcus that upon arrival a servant greets them. He speaks little Latin but seems more familiar with speaking Greek. Petrus has, more or less, forgotten his school Greek, but somehow he understands the servant requesting them to come inside whilst he prepares food. He said that the master is not in the house but will arrive later.

Whilst waiting for the food to be prepared, they notice the owner's taste in Greek literature and see many small many paintings relating to ancient Greek tales. On floors are many thick Greek woven wool rugs on and the servant has lit a fire.

The servant then serves them with a superb meal and excellent wine.

Marcus briefly tells them about the house where they are staying. Lucy and Petrus agree that they will continue to stay in the house with all its comforts which belong to the Greek unknown host, even though in the wrong house.

Marcus on leaving says, 'Oh do not be surprised if you see Julia looking six months pregnant. Just don't say a word. I will explain when we all get back at the wagon in the morning.'

When Marcus returns to the house of the senator's friends, he tells them the news about Petrus and Lucy staying at the wrong house.

They explain to Marcus the reason for their small amount of furniture. 'We sold our farm here which now forms part of a collection of small farms that are being run on a large scale by slaves and with an owner living in Rome. I gather the owner is a senator, but do not know his name. We were not making much profit and paying tax, which senators do not have to do, forcing us to sell. We do not know how we are to earn a living after we move away,' comments the host.

'The coast is lovely so I'm sure you'll enjoy it there. I was thinking of expanding my business,' says Julie.

She explains the importing and exporting and asks if they would like to sell some of her products when they have settled down at the coast. He says that he would like to be included in the business venture.

'We will certainly keep in touch when we settle in at the coast. I am sure that you are tired and need to rest before your journey tomorrow.'

'We're sorry that the bedroom is a little sparse.'

Eventually they go to bed, not daring to say that they are not married.

Julia and Marcus, the co-called married couple, are eventually alone in the double bedroom. They are too tired to argue on which side of the bed to sleep.

It is difficult to move in the bed because it is old and rickety with one leg shorter than the other three legs. The bed had a tendency to wobble with the slightest movement. They have only one blanket and they cuddled their bodies together for warmth.

Early in the morning, Marcus awakes to find himself with one leg over the top of Julia. She subconsciously believed she had been cuddling up to blankets, as she does in her own bed at home. Lying on her back and not noticing that Marcus' leg is placed over her body.

Slowly he moves and Julia moved much closer.

It was comforting for both to be alone together and needing each other.

Now his body was far more alert. At times, it operates on its own volition without much mental control. They are in a moment of silent pleasure, yet trying not to rock the bed leg, which seemed to want to join in with the motion, when suddenly, approaching footsteps can be heard. Julia pulls up the blanket over their naked bodies.

The host walks in with a hot drink.

Marcus can barely speak – as the drinks are placed on the single table by the bed. 'Thank you,' says Julie. The host departs.

A few minutes earlier Marcus felt like a hero warrior on a galloping horse ready to leap across a bridge – suddenly his drawbridge is pulled up – a sudden stop – and the exciting illusion of the moment is lost. He feels crushed – all for the sake of a morning drink.

'Are you going to let me have a share of either the blanket or the shawl to save me leaping across the room naked,' he asks.

'No – I remember last evening on the roadside – you had your backside in my face whilst you straddled my body with your legs – trying to shove a shawl into my tiny bikini briefs, if I recall.'

'There was a reason – I was trying hurriedly to make you pregnant.'

'I think you got the wrong end of the stick – your backside is not supposed to be by my face' she says jokingly.

'Naked it has to be,' he mutters, as he crosses the room to find his clothes.

Giving a dignified leap across the room and showing off his physique was his intention, but his ankle was still sore, which took away all dignity as he hobbled on one foot.

Julia went off into fits of laughter.

'Now you have seen it all – I'm a man with nothing to hide.'

*

Gorgias

Not long after Petrus and Lucy have eaten and spoken with Marcus, they sit comfortably in front of a warm fire when an elderly man opens the door to join them. 'Welcome to my home. I am Gorgias.'

Petrus explains the whole story – and their apologies for the confusion. He explains to Gorgias that it was only after they had eaten that they understood that they were in the wrong house.

'I am from an old Greek family and we always make guests welcome. I don't live in this house much, because of my failing eyesight, and my old neighbourly friend reads my favourite books to me.

'My friend lives just a few houses away. He looks after me and we have enjoyed each other's companionship over many years. I hope that you get the chance to meet him.'

'I have only seen a portion of your farm, but it looks a great place to live,' said Petrus.

Gorgias replies, 'I don't know what I will do with the farm as I am growing too old to keep it functioning properly. I would hate to see my loyal slaves being sold with my farm. But, I am being harassed by some new neighbours, who want me to get off my land,' he pauses.

'They buy up lots of farms in the area, and there are local farmers who have been selling their farms, for small sums of money. They now live in poverty, as they cannot earn a living, except to become slaves themselves.

'My health has been poor, and my servant tells me of troubles being created by my new neighbours. It seems that they have moved the recognised marker which defines our boundaries. With the border marker removed, my fruit trees now appear to be on his land.'

'Did you sign any documents for him to have the land?'

'He said that I had signed a document selling my land to him.'

'Had you signed?'

'No.'

'How did he get hold of your signature?'

'Well, it took me some time to wonder about that myself. Then I remembered that he had sent forms to everyone in the area to share the payments for repairs to a communal road. We all signed the form. The road is not on my land, but a little further away, but we all use it to get to market.

'I think that the scoundrel of a man, must have copied my signature from that document saying that I had sold him the land.

'To dispute it, means that I shall have to go to court which is several miles away, to fight my case. The scoundrel has plenty of money to delay court cases. I can imagine myself making a long journey to court – and then on the date the case is to be heard, find that the case is cancelled. I understand from other farmers that this can be repeated many times. One the other hand, I could lose part of my farm if do not take action.

'I am just an elderly man, and the courts are over-packed. The men who have money can use their influence in the courts to have dates and hours altered on the last minute – knowing full well the inconvenience it causes their opponents.'

Lawyers acting for wealthy individuals create false reasons to delay cases. Trumped up reasons such as a lawyer has left a file in his office some distance away, or that he must make a visit to the toilet also some distance away – all these delaying tactics increase his fees. Leaving a defendant having to find time and money to attend a different court date and pay more money to his own lawyer.'

Petrus placed his hand on the old man's shoulder. 'Have you any relatives?'

'Yes, I have a son. I have written letters to him but have not received any replies.'

'I will send one of my surveyors from Rome to help you with your boundary problems. This is a thank you for your generosity.'

'He seems a wise man, yet sad,' comments Lucy after Gorgias had returned to his neighbour's house to sleep.

Lucy decides not to sleep in the bedroom but chooses to sleep in front of the fire. She looks at the scrolls on the shelves which Gorgias had read in earlier times before his failing eyesight. One is written by the poet Protagoras and another by Philostratos.

Petrus takes the scrolls away from Lucy. 'These are works by Sophists and far too difficult for you to understand so late in the evening. The Sophists enjoyed Greek rhetoric and arguments. Certainly, not bedtime reading for my lovely Lucy.'

Petrus considers that no matter how many books Gorgias read in the past about the Sophists, and their cleverness of arguments – it does not help Gorgias in court appearance when lawyers choose delaying tactics which causes him stress in his older years and loss of money.

Petrus chose for Lucy a book of love poems by the Roman poet Propertius.

He tells Lucy, 'Propertius' poetry was addressed to a woman named Cynthia. Nobody knows whether Cynthia was a real person or whether she existed in his imagination. But it is about emotion and desire.' Petrus places the book next to her.

He looks around the house to find some cushions and a blanket for his head, and when he returns Lucy is nearly asleep and the book has fallen on the floor. Petrus places a blanket on her and gives her a kiss on her forehead.'

'Sleep well my lovely.'

With that she gently places her hand to his face, and dreamily says, 'Thank you for looking after me today. I think I love you.'

'I love you also, my sweet.' But she does not hear him ... she is in a deep sleep after a tiring journey.

Before leaving in the morning, Petrus and the old man walked around the farm. Petrus notices that there are a few hectares of land on the southern side of the farm overlooking Terracina that belongs to Gorgias. The land had not been affected by the eruption of Vitruvius, which took place several years earlier, and is fertile and full of grapevines that have been sadly neglect but still bearing grapes.

Gorgias points to his fruit trees that have now become part of the neighbouring farmer's land, and not providing access for Gorgias to pick his own fruit.

Walking back across the farm, the old man speaks of the ancient Roman god *Terminus*.

'Do you remember Ovid's story, written at the beginning of the Empire, about the ancient god *Terminus*?'

Before Petrus can reply the old man continues. 'The god defined the separation of land between two owners with either a tree stump buried in the ground, or a stone, as markers. When this was initially carried out, the owners would each bring a cake and garland as a physical act of honouring the god *Terminus*.'

'The last king of Rome, Tarquinius Superbus, wanted a temple on the Capitol dedicated to the god *Jupiter*. Shrines were removed to make way for the new temple, except that of *Terminus*. The god's boundary marker remains in place, not hidden and out of sight, but with an opening to the sky that is *Terminus*' demarcation point.'

When they are ready to depart, Petrus said to Gorgias, 'I will always be grateful for your kindness and hospitality. Lucy and I have made a new friend.

'My surveyor will be sent to you after I reach Rome, with instructions to help you with your problems.'

Petrus, after noticing that Gorgias has the works of Protagoras and Philostratus in his possession, believes that Gorgias in his younger years would have gone to court to fight his case, as he shows himself to have had the mentally and verbally capability to win. But Gorgias' in his older years he no longer has the stamina to spend hours sitting in court, and travelling there on a rickety wagon which Petrus had noticed earlier, as it was positioned close to the house.

As they departed they were sorry to leave. It was so tranquil, with the noise of the goats in the distance, birds can be heard singing or calling each other, and there is a smell of flower blossoms.

They make their way back to join Julia and Marcus at the wagon, which now has a fresh horse and everyone is ready to leave for Ostia, and finally up the Tiber to Rome.

On their return journey, they all tell their stories – but Marcus and Julia do not mention that they had shared a bed.

CHAPTER EIGHT

Crispus Returns to Rome

Crispus' father had died before his arrival at the main farm. He had left all his estate to Crispus. There is no wife or children to cause him trouble.

It was a long time ago when he last looked around his father's farms. The farm manager, who is very efficient, offers to show him around all the changes that had been made during his absence. The manager had also made funeral arrangements and invited mourners.

After all the stress that Crispus believes he has suffered, it was pleasant to go around and see the land where his father and grandfather had made their livelihoods.

He notices that a man, who oversees the vegetable farm is showing features similar to his father. He begins to wonder if his thoughts are running awry.

Surely his father did not have intercourse with the women slaves on the farms.

Three fruit pickers are working on the next farm, he stares at their faces. Perhaps he is tired, but he cannot stop himself from searching their features to see if they also bear any characteristics to his father, and worse perhaps having features like his own.

He is afraid to look closely at their children – surely not generations of his father being passed on down the line. It is making him stressed and glad to walk away from the farms, and back to the main house.

Upon reaching the main house he looks closely at the eyes, mouth and ears, and features of older slave workers who are clearing leaves. He desperately tries to remember what his grandfather looked like. Happily he is relieved to see that the farm manager and the workers looks nothing like his grandfather, father, or himself.

Now that he is on the way to becoming a man of wealth, he vows that he will stay loyal to his wife. Desiring the appearance of an aristocrat, he makes up his mind to purchase a very large dwelling in Rome.

Petrus must be given instructions to quickly find him an impressive house with a swimming pool – one that suits his new status. He does not like to swim, but it is the impression that counts.

*

Rufus and arrival of Anna

Ndio, upon Julia and Marcus' return to Rome, notices that they gently touch each other when speaking, and laugh a lot together.

Whilst thinking of Marcus, he unexpectedly, appears in the showroom with a small package. 'Please give this to Julia and tell her that I will meet her later at Sextus' house.'

She thought that it was probably to do with work as he had mentioned the house of Sextus. Perhaps it was to do with the pond and the statue of the goddess Diana.

She saw a note on the parcel which read: "A small present of a shawl to wrap around you – I'm available to assist"!

Ndio thought he was a bit cheeky. Julia always knows how to dress properly and look smart and attractive.

He starts to leave the showroom when a sedan chair stops outside and out steps a very attractive woman who enters the showroom. Ndio notices her orange-red hair.

But just as the woman begins to speak, Marcus creeps up quietly behind her and places his hands across her eyes. 'Guess who?'

'I know it's you Marcus.'

He gives her a close and very friendly hug.

She gives him a scroll, and on the outside Ndio can see a seal with a tiny picture of bird with an open mouth.

After they speak a few quiet words together – he departs. 'See you later for dinner this evening.'

Ndio has a dilemma – should she tell Julia or just remain silent. She is unaware that Anna had been staying at Sextus' house for a few days upon arrival.

Hardly has Ndio recovered, when she has a surprise visit from her friend who has returned earlier from Frejus in France and wants to tell her the latest news.

She said that it was exciting to see the empty amphitheatre in Frejus, and the aqueduct, and loved seeing the harbour and walk along the beach.

But apart from being taken on that visit, she was generally at madam's beck-and-call and only spoke with other servants at the house where they stayed, but she did have a little gossip for Ndio.

'My madam has brought some friends back to Rome with her where they will holiday for a few days. The man, wife and their daughter Samara, know Marcus. He has stayed with them in France.

'The other workers at the house in France told me that they overheard my Madam saying that Marcus is about to inherit lots of money because he is going to run all his uncle's businesses.

'It seems that the French family now want their daughter will meet up with Marcus again and that perhaps he will marry Samara.'

'That's interesting', comments Ndio. Who now wonders whether the red-haired woman who came into the showroom earlier is Samara from France?

Madam was outside the showroom and furiously calling for her maid. Leaving Ndio with questions and nobody to answer them.

When Julia arrives at Sextus' house late afternoon, she notices another carriage at the entrance.

Marcus greets her with a cheeky grin – 'I am always available to help you with a shawl.'

As she was laughing, he drew her to one side.

'There are two friends of mine from London. They are involved in exporting. Rufus is into metal work such as lamps and his sister Anna sells small silver jewellery that she designs. They are planning to buy an apartment here for importing and exporting their wares. I thought you may like to meet them. They may be able to represent you in London, which is where I met them.'

'Was she an ex-girlfriend?'

'Yes. More a close friend, than girlfriend. But now she is engaged to be married to an Italian who lives in London.'

'Perhaps you may be interested in placing some of their jewellery or lanterns in your showroom?'

During the evening Julia notices Anna is slightly flirting with Marcus, but he has more interest in talking about wines and conversing with Rufus about the business.

When they leave, Marcus asks Julia to stay, as there is another business matter that he wishes to discuss with her. They walk in the garden and towards the pond.

'You know I want to marry you, if you will have me forever.'

'Of course, forever – I would love nothing better.'

'It must wait until Sextus has handed over the business. Not because I need his money because I can survive on what I already had – but because I do not want to take away his moment of joy. It is giving him a thrill to take an interest in what I am going to do with his business, but when all has settled then we will marry.

'In the meantime, I will look for a ring – not a simple wedding ring, and then you can tell me if it meets with your approval – or you can reject it.'

'Why would I reject anything you give me?'

'Well it's a challenge for me. Did you like the scarf?'

'I understood that the scarf was a suggestion to spend another night in bed with me just wearing a scarf!'

'I loved what I saw – and a lot without scarf.'

She playfully started to hit him on his arm – when suddenly Sextus appeared.

'What are you two up to?'

'I am trying my hardest to be sweet and charming, whilst she is being very rude to me. In fact, trying to hit me.'

Sextus quickly picks on the fact that they are very much in love yet pretending not to be.

'Crispus' wife has returned to Rome with some friends who know you Marcus. A woman named Samara and her parents,' says Sextus.

'In a couple of days' time, I will be holding my last wine tasting gathering. Hopefully everyone will attend and, Julia perhaps you and Lucy can help with one or two stands to tell the guests about our marvellous wines that we have imported or exported.'

'Look forward to it,' says Julia to Sextus as he returns to the house.

Marcus reluctantly tells Julia all about his visit to the chateau in France and the weaponry on the walls ... and his hasty retreat.

'Well perhaps we can put this all to good use,' Julia comments. 'I just want to see you squirm when the father brings a lance with him to the wine showing.'

'One squirming woman is quite enough for me.' He gave her a hug. 'It's going to be a little embarrassing, but I will just try and be charming.'

'But tonight's guests will be Anna and Rufus, and of course Papinus.'

They walk around the pond to see if there is any more work to be carried out. The ground around the pond now has plants beginning to grow, and there are a few yellow and pink water lilies growing in the pond. The statues are in place.

The wooden carvings of dogs are in position around a few trees, and a wooden stag is facing the pond. Sextus' marble benches have been placed in position, and a carved wooden dog sits nearby on its hindquarters as if waiting for a titbit.

'I would like to have a small path leading down from the mansion down to the pond which will be easy for Sextus to walk along. Perhaps you may remember our conversation when I mentioned that if your client Sextus requests more work for your business, that my reward is a dinner from you and Lucy.'

'Of course, I will keep that promise, and we'll invite Petrus and Lucy to join us. It will be in my house that Lucy and I share, but it will be a simple meal.'

*

Crispus' House Search

Crispus does not have much time for his wife's guests from France. He is more interested in finding a mansion to his liking. He is not going to tell his wife until he can complete the deal and give her a surprise.

He quickly departs from his wife and his visitors and makes his way to Petrus' office.

Messalina is walking towards his house and stops him.

'Do you like my silk shawl, which I have just bought in the market?'

It gives him a quick shock to be seen with her and her cloak or shawl. The garment is made of bright silk pieces of silk, as if off-cuts from a tailor's sack.

'Do you like it?'

'I was wondering whether you bought it when travelling on the ancient Silk Road, at a remarkably low price. Perhaps the mythological king, Sardanapalus, was the original owner?'

'Do you like all the bright colours?' she asks, thinking he was passing her a compliment.

'Just wear what you like ... it's none of my business,' he retorts.

Crispus is more interested in his plans, and told Messalina that they can meet in a few days' time.

As an aspiring aristocrat, he does not wish to have her tagging around with him.

I shall arrange a dinner party and let you know the date.

With that he hurries away.

Crispus is barely interested. His attention is directed towards meeting Petrus who can show him some great mansions with pools, and fine gardens with a prospect of buying one.

*

Reading the constellations

Anna and Rufus are settling in at Papinus' barn house. Rufus is spending most of his days with Sextus, learning how to increase his business in Britain by export lamps and metal jewellery, such as pendants, amulets and pins and broaches.

Anna interests are in designing, so she spends her time drawing and using the materials that Tullio has left behind. 'You are welcome to use them,' says Papinus. 'Tullio never paid for the art material.'

Julia had mentioned to Anna, when they met at Sextus' house, that people are interested in paintings for their homes. Anna is now inspired to paint pictures of fruit and portraits. People like to have portraits on their walls and these do not have to look like any of their descendants or themselves. It is a wall decoration.

Papinus and Anna work as a team, he prepares the panels for her work and mixes her paints and sometimes fills in some of the background scenery.

Her paintings begin to stack up against the walls of the barn ready for Julia to take a quick look – hopefully ready for either the showroom or sending with other goods of Julia's for packaging by sea. It is now a race against time before the last of the ships sail and winter sets in.

Both Papinus and Anna enjoy each other's company. At the end of each tiring day, they enjoy a meal together consisting of fresh produce from the farm, which Felix skilfully organizes.

Papinus now finds himself growing more drawn towards Anna – but perhaps he is a little too old and she would prefer a younger man – so he holds back on his feelings and emotion.

Anna has written to the man in London whom she has promised to marry, to say that she will not be returning and that she has grown closer to someone else.

It was now a pleasant warm evening with a clear sky. They sit outside looking up at the stars.

He places his arm on Anna's shoulder and touches her hand indicating areas in the sky, and pointing out particular stars.

Papinus is taking pleasure in relating the stories of the ancient gods and heroes up in the sky. 'Let me tell you about some of the constellations and the Greek myths.'

Pointing to the northern sky, he outlines the constellation of *Perseus*, who wore winged boots.

'The tale of *Perseus*, who was semi-divine, was born as a result of the god *Zeus* and mortal *Danaë*. She had been kept in a cellar by her father, but *Zeus* transformed himself into a golden shower, came into the room and entered her womb.'

'*Zeus* seems to have crept into a lot of wombs,' says Anna.

Papinus then shows Anna the constellations of heroic *Perseus* and *Andromeda* and remembers that Corinna liked this story. Then he points out the constellations of Hercules, and the Gemini, being the twins supposedly being Castor and Pollux.

Papinus believes that the gods are present, as he stands behind Anna looking up at the sky and pointing out the stars, with their bodies touching. She turns around and kisses him.

'Tell me more about these ancient gods.'

He is enjoying this intimacy, and was happy to continue.

'Follow my fingers and you can see in the constellation ... but his words become lost in their passionate embrace.'

Anna can smell his hair and he can taste her lipstick when they kiss. There are no servants around and they lie down upon the grass. Her head is resting on his shoulder, and as he moves on top of her ready to kiss her again, she gives a loud yelp.

The broach on her right shoulder has loosened from the clasp as he leans against her. It jabs into her shoulder. She shows him what had happened and he quickly takes it off her shoulder and throws it on the ground.

'Quickly,' he says, 'get on your knees and search for it.'

'Why?'

'Because, there are times when may you want a slave, and times when you do not. This is that moment. My servant is making his way here to see if there is a problem.'

'Are you all right,' asks Felix.

'We're fine thanks. The madam lost her broach – but we have found it, but thank you for coming.'

Papinus and Anna go into the house, and must wait for another evening when they have the grounds to themselves.

The servant wakes up some of the other servants and they have a big discussion among themselves, to try and find an explanation, and to reason what really happened.

Was he attacking her. Was she attacking him. Did he get amorous?

Oh, this reminded them of the good days of Corinna. This was going to bring excitement back into their evenings.

*

Tasting the wine

The work on Sextus' pond is finally finished. The fountain spouts out water when a lever is pressed on the furthest side of the pond, to make it seem that Diana, the goddess is spraying water onto those on the opposite bank. The spray only lasts for a few seconds – just to make it a surprise.

The benches, which previously belonged to Papinus, are near to the lake and facing towards where the sunlight comes through the trees.

Between the trees the ground is flattened to create earthen pathways, for people to stroll along. Plants have been chosen to grow near the trees and a few small deer made from carved wooden and carved dogs make the walk interesting.

Invitations are sent out to merchants, connoisseurs or wine growers who wish to exhibit their products.

Marcus personally sends out the invitation to the French girl, Samara, and her parents, as well as Crispus and his wife.

About twenty-years earlier, Sextus he had an area of land, approximately five hectares, standing idle. He appointed Fabius, the architect, to design a large wine cellar. Soon after approving Fabius' designs, the construction and the land around, began to take shape.

Fabius, whom he had recently met again at the Circus Maximus is also invited to the wine tasting.

When the early work on the cellar was first completed, everyone was quite excited, and still are – with its four barrel-arched tunnels with ceilings that are semi-circular, and the tunnels which run north, south, east, west, meeting at the centre with a groin vaulted ceiling and marble pillars for supports. Along the length of each tunnel are niches where the wine can be tested.

Outside its main entrance Fabius placed soil, that had been removed from the foundations to create a mini amphitheatre, and a stage platform next to the entrance, so that if there are several people wanting to know which districts or country where the wine has come from, they can sit whilst Sextus, Marcus or their employees can tell them more about the vines growing in a particular area or country.

After talking about wines, the guests can recline at the amphitheatre where Sextus likes to organize performances of Greek or Roman satires.

Fabius designed the amphitheatre in recognition of the ancient Greeks, around the time of the Fifth century. Their plays were sacred and the god *Dionysus* was not only connected to the playwrights and awards at the amphitheatres, but the god was also known for his association with vines.

Fabius allows a space close to the stage, for a throne so that a statue of the god can be placed on the throne whenever a play is about to begin and a toast raised in his honour.

Julia, Lucy and Marcus, organize temporary pergolas around the grounds where wines are on display.

*

Samara arrives with her parents. Julia stands a few paces further away just to watch Marcus in anticipation of his embarrassment. But Samara's father pulls Marcus over to one side and walks with him a short distance away from everyone else.

'I know that you left my chateau a little hastily, and I can understand.'

'Oh, it was my fault for knocking on the wrong door.'

'No, no. I was quite a relief to see that it was you. I thought you were my wife catching me in a compromising situation. Well, perhaps a little more than compromising.'

He pauses. 'I have been having an affair with my wife's stepsister. A rather attractive woman, with soft, silky skin.' He pauses as if in a trance.

Marcus slightly raises his eyebrows. He saw Julia looking at him waiting for Samara's father to punch him because of the chateau situation.

Samara's father continues. 'I have never met a woman like her – when she walks into the bedroom with her silk gown and long legs – I feel as if in a dream. I just can't give her up. I can't tell my wife. I can't tell my daughter. Such a dilemma.'

Turning to Marcus – 'You are a man of the world – what would you advise?'

Marcus was still trying to understand the ways of Julia, and did not consider himself to be a man full of wisdom on domestic matters. But made a small effort to proffer what little thought he could give on the matter.

'I think that you, and the beautiful, long-legged woman, are enjoying what you have … perhaps she is your dream woman, or perhaps it is the enjoyment of the risk and the danger of being caught. My advice is to just continue enjoying these moments whilst you can. The memories will last you a lifetime.'

'Thank you so much – I am so pleased that we have met to discuss this. You are welcome to visit the chateau again.'

'Well now that you are here – perhaps you may be interested in starting up a sort of franchise by selling our products in Arles. If you have premises in the town, then perhaps you might like to stock our wines from Sicily and various parts of Italy and Greece. The ships will be taking the amphora when the weather improves for sailing.'

'I should like that very much.'

'Sextus is somewhere around – ask him to give you a packet of picture cards. He likes to give them to his best customers – his little secret packets.'

Marcus had a laugh when he left the man.

Julia walks up to Marcus. 'How was your meeting?'

'Oh, we just discussed manly things like wine and if he will represent us in Arles.'

'Well I have been talking with Samara and she says that she wants to marry her cousin, and hopes that her mother and father will agree.'

'Which cousin – I did meet one of two.'

'I didn't ask.'

Marcus hopes it was not the stepson of Lycus' wife.

Lucy asks Marcus what the play in the amphitheatre is about, as she notices people picking up cushions and getting themselves seated.

'It's called "The Brothers Menaechmus". The comedy was written by the Roman playwright Plautus.

'He begins his plays by telling the audience a story which is about Greeks who live in Syracuse, Sicily.

'It's about a young boy, Menaechmus, the eldest of twin boys. He is taken by his father to a fair in Tarentum, a coastal town lying of the foot of Italy. He becomes lost and a wealthy merchant, who is visiting the fair in Tarentum, finds the lost boy and takes him back to live with him at Epidamnus, a town across the Adriatic Sea, opposite the east coast of Italy. When the wealthy merchant dies he leaves the elder twin, Menaechmus, all his money.

'The stage is set showing Menaechmus' house where he lives with his wife, a road to the port, and in the next house lives Menaechmus' courtesan mistress with her attendants.

'Menaechmus steals his wife's robe to give to his mistress so that she can entertain him by providing wine and food later that day.

'But the Greeks in the audience are aware that a Greek husband owns all what his wife possesses, so Menaechmus is really stealing from himself. He then goes into town with his friend Peniculus, who is a man who likes to sponge off people, and who manages to get an invitation to join Menaechmus and the mistress when the food has been prepared.

'The younger twin, Socicles, accompanied by his slave, has searched many ports to find his older brother, and eventually arrives at the port town Epidamnus.'

'Before leaving Sicily his dying grandfather, said that Socicles should keep the name, Menaechmus, on-going, and requested the younger twin to have the same name as the older twin – and because of this request both brothers now have the same name.'

'His slave, who is more street wise, says that he will go back to the boat to sort out some things, but he will take the purse as he thinks the port town is full of harlots and rogues.

'The younger twin Socicles/Manaechmus ventures further towards the house, which is owned by the courtesan, Erotium.

'From then onwards the younger twin is mistaken for the older brother and mistaken identity brings about lots of fun and humour. It is the slave who shows that he is wise and has to inform the brothers that they are twins.

'Plautus, the Roman writer of the play, had lived in Sicily at the time when Hannibal was there and then departed. Plautus understood the humour enjoyed by both Romans and Greeks.'

CHAPTER NINE

Plans for a Trojan War Party

It is the time of the year when the senator holds a weekend birthday party.

The theme is always based on the game of the Trojan War. But because of the number of people and work involved, he only holds the party every second year.

The senator's country house outside Rome is situated between his two farms. His friends stay either in the main house or, on his large farm on the right-hand side of a river. The friends take on the roles of the Achaean/Greeks, keep their clothing and warrior equipment in a storeroom at the farm.

Gundher's work is to send invitations to the senator's close friends. He likes to write out the invitations with a copper pen on vellum. The first letter of each paragraph beginning with a gold or red coloured letter, and the rest of the wording in black ink, from China. Gundher chooses to write on the inner-skin side of the vellum, which although it is slightly darker, there are no hairs.

Guests can later re-use these invitations or epistles, should they wish, by rubbing out the writing. The vellum being re-useable. Or turned over to use the vellum on the hair side. It is expensive writing material.

The Trojans guests, who are mainly Julia's friends, will be based on the senator's smaller farm, with its own house and outbuildings situation on the left-hand side of the river.

Everyone knows the routine, except for Julia's friends. The senator has invited Papinus, who normally attends these games, to inform the Trojan guests about the event.

Papinus' writing material, for the invitations to Julia's friends, will not be on expensive vellum. The sheepskin of a young animal has been made into parchment, and costing a little less than the vellum.

A bone shaped pen and powdered Indian ink is used by Papinus. Often the powdered ink will thicken and come out as a blob – fortunately mistakes can be erased. He likes to write on the outer skin side, as do most Italians, but sometimes there are several hairs. The hairs can prevent the writer from forming certain letters of the alphabet. Such as when writing the letter 'I" it could become an 'L' when, a hair from the animal skin crosses the lower portion of the lettering.

Papinus gives out a list to each person on the rules and conditions for the Trojan War party. Each guest shall be required to wear Trojan masks, or tribal masks of that period, wear black clothing, and carry weaponry of that period. The weapons are not dangerous as they are made of soft wood and a variety of other materials. All the clothing will be provided at the farm marked with a sign saying 'TROAS' on the back.

The TROAS will be positioned in the farmhouse and properties on the left-hand side of the river.

The right-hand side of the river is supposed to be where the Achaean/Greek campsite is positioned. They need to be situated close to their ships. Between this part of the river is a small oxbow where is a bend before a bridge, then further downstream the water becomes shallower.

Guests are expected to stay on their respective sides of the river, except for fighting scenes, and on the very last day they all get together on the Achaean/Greek side for a competition to choose the best athletic warrior. The event will finish with a huge bonfire, feasting and entertainment.

Everyone needs to arrive early on Saturday because the game will begin at midday. Saturday's game event will continue until early evening when each side will have its own food and entertainment.

Sunday, after breakfast, the game will continue and stop for a lunch break. After a mid-day meal, everyone will return to the same positions they held on the battlefield. Then the war continues until early evening, when the game finishes.

Guests can either leave on Sunday evening after the end of the games – or they are welcome to stay on the farms until Monday morning.

Upon receiving their invitations Lycus and Honey-Bee quickly make their plans to be in Rome. Honey-Bee has been told that she will be the goddess *Aphrodite* – the most beautiful woman, and Lycus playing the part of *Paris*.

He thinks it would all be fun because he knows the story of *Paris*, and that the character will be spending a lot of time in the palace with *Helen* of

Troy and is excited at the thought of who would be chosen as *Helen* and imagines a little amorous liaison.

Honey-bee does not know the story of the Trojan war, but she did not reveal this to Lycus. She believes that *Aphrodite* is *Helen*. Meaning that she will play the most attractive woman being taken by *Paris* to Troy.

Quintus, the senator, and his old friends, the consul and Dio the writer, meet at the farm to discuss the arrangements for the war party. It would be the same routine as in past years. But they often change their roles, and sometimes brought in others when they were short and needed a place to be filled.

The senator, tells his friends, 'Julia has now collected a few friends of her own. Therefore, I have asked Papinus to invite them all to take the side of the Trojans. It will give us a chance to meet this next generation because in a few years' time they may be playing on our side, as Achaean/Greeks. We will be able to judge each person, see which ones can stand up to the mettle.'

'So what role are you going to play this year?'

Quintus replies, 'I have decided to play *Achilles* – I can then sit it out for most of the time, until I need to fight *Hector*, prince of the Trojans – and then I can have a good fight.'

'Have you decided who will play *Hector*?'

'Yes, it will be Julia's boyfriend, Marcus, who has intentions of marrying my daughter. I do not want some wimp becoming her husband. This will be his chance to prove himself.'

'Does he know this yet?'

'No, it will be the element of surprise. I will let him and Julia know on the last minute.'

'Should be interesting. Suddenly this war game, of the ancient Achaean/Greeks versus the Trojans, takes on a whole new meaning.'

'We are all looking forward to it. We'll keep the bandages at the ready.'

Dio says that he wants to be chosen for the role of king *Agamemnon*.

The consul say that he will take on the role of *Diomedes*, because he fancies having a helmet that can shoot fire, and having a special visor to see the gods and goddesses and differentiate them from the humans.

'Well I do not want real fire shooting out, I don't want my head burnt.'

'No, it won't be as dangerous – just jagged red pieces of papyrus, to make it look like fire.'

*

Somnium domum – A dream house

Petrus manages to find Crispus the house of his dreams. The entrance is through the gates and a large garden with plants, paths, trees leading to the frontage of the house with its marble slabs and pots on either side supporting medium height trees.

Just the entrance alone impresses Crispus as he looks up at the residence with its triple storey frontage showing six tall pillars and a portico, which is just what Crispus desires.

Petrus leads him into the inner, courtyard, and passing by several rooms on either side.

The central courtyard has a garden area, and an altar in the centre with a small fountain, and one or two figurines of gods.

As Crispus looks around he can see there are rooms on the ground and upper floors, with staircases either side.

On the downstairs level, from the courtyard on the right is a large room leading out to a privately enclosed swimming pool that has a door leading out to communal gardens surrounding the house.

Crispus immediately says that he will take the place. He likes the idea of a large study that is situated on the left side of the entrance, and he feels that he is close to all the activity, if he were positioned close to all the rooms on the left of the buildings. He also likes the garden area on that side of the mansion.

He decides that his wife can have the right-hand side, as place to entertain her friends, and she can have the swimming pool area, because he does not like swimming.

'How are you going to pay for this property,' asks Petrus, 'because I can then arrange a meeting with the banker and confer with the owner. We can conclude the business when all documents and monies have been exchanged.

'The owner wants to retire to the coast. I am sure that you could make some arrangements with him if you wish to take over his servants.'

Crispus replies, 'I think I shall take out a loan on the property. I will to go over the profits of my father's farms and, if they are good, then I will pay a small amount in cash, but first I think it's wise to take out a loan so that the deal can take place as quickly as possible.'

'If you borrow, the interest rate will be at twelve per cent.'

'That's all right.'

Crispus has a plan in his mind, to stick down a small deposit, then he will apply for a loan drawn up in his wife's name. Get her to sign it, with her believing that they both have to repay on the loan, but each one separately – when in fact she would be paying back all the loan.

He was enjoying the moment and being back to his old ways of finding the excitement and challenging his wife.

He used to steal her silver and ornaments to pay for his huge meals and entertainment. Now, he is planning bigger things. She will be paying off the entire loan and he can still help himself to the silver.

The problem with the plan is trying to get his wife to sign the loan document for the loan repayment. He needs to find a moment when she is busy with guests – quickly put the document in front of her, show annoyance and complain and argue with her – making her feel uncomfortable with her friends close by – this will cause her to dither and sign just to be rid of him.

After a few days, Petrus presents him with the document in its final form and only needing signatures. Crispus says, 'Oh you have left out my wife's name. She actually wants to take out the whole loan herself after I have secured the deal with a small deposit.'

'I will get the document altered, and indicate which pages she needs to sign.'

On the strength of all his manoeuvring. Crispus takes Messalina out for dinner at an expensive local tavern.

A few more days pass and Crispus wonders what is happening, because Petrus is taking a long time drawing up the contract, and Crispus is afraid of losing the house.

But Crispus' wife has already made contact with Petrus.

She decides to find out the facts, about the plan to purchase a house, from Petrus. Her maid had overheard Crispus talking with a man about the cost of moving furniture and mentioning that he was moving into a larger house. Of course the maid informed her mistress, who checked Crispus' diary and noticed his meetings with Petrus regarding the purchase of a house.

Petrus explains the situation to Crispus' wife – that her husband wants to keep it a surprise, but explains that her signature is needed on the documents.

She now realises that she will be the one signing the repayments on the house. But notices upon reading the document that her husband had manipulated the purchase giving her the debt and himself sole ownership. She realises that he makes it appear to Petrus that she is gifting her husband the property.

'I don't know much about buying a property, but is it subject to the first person who pays the money buys the house?'

'Well something like that,' replies Petrus. 'Your husband needs to act swiftly as it really is a good property in a good area. Otherwise someone else can put in an offer and then you will lose it.'

'In that case, I will act swiftly and buy it right now.'

'What, without your husband – without taking out a loan?'

'Yes, I have inheritance money left to me by my family, so I am of independent means. Can you arrange the money transfers as soon as possible?'

'Yes, we can complete the documents this morning, and meet with the bankers and the person representing the sellers, and if all goes well, the house will be yours.'

'Well, let's get started.'

'Look forward to completing the deal,' says Petrus. Not knowing whether the wife is going to surprise her husband at his birthday. It is not for him to understand marriage relationships. Business is business.

Two weeks pass by before Crispus returns to Petrus' office.

'Sorry not to get back to you, but my wife has been a difficult woman to speak with these days, to get her to sign a loan document.' He lies about speaking with his wife.

'The house has been sold,' said Petrus.

Crispus' colour drains from his face – a mixture of rage and shock.

'Who has purchased it?'

'Well your wife came in and signed the documents and paid the money, so she is the owner. She said that this would be your surprise and in return she will let you buy all the furnishing.

Crispus cannot believe that she has turned the tables on him. She knows that he has been stealing items from their previous dwelling to pay for his expensive meals. Now he can steal anything he wishes, because all the furniture and ornaments now belong solely to him, and there's no fun in cheating any more.

Again, Crispus is suffering and grasps the arms of the chair he is sitting in.

Breaking the ice – Petrus says – 'Aren't you a lucky man ... having a good wife and a lovely new home?'

Crispus did not feel like a lucky man

He mutters something to himself and leaves.

*

Petrus receives news from his surveyor to say that Gorgias' boundary markers are now officially in place and he has his fruit trees are back on his own land.

At the same time, he has managed to track down Gorgias' son who was living on his father-in-law's farm with his wife and child.

The son came to visit his father and has agreed to bring his family to live with his father, and help to bring the vineyard back to its original state.

Petrus is pleased that his surveyor had worked so well to bring the family together.

As a thank you Petrus he wrote back to the surveyor: 'Please buy a mule and cart for Gorgias for being so kind and hospitable.'

It was not for just spending a night at the elderly man's house, but whilst he was there he made up his mind to marry Lucy. Gorgias' kind hospitality had made a special impression on his own life. He will be visiting his parents at Baiae in December and will take her with him and make plans for marriage. Of course he will first ask permission from Quintus who is her guardian.

It was the kindly act by Gorgias and his hospitality, that made Petrus return the kindness.

CHAPTER TEN

Trojan War Party

Saturday morning is busy at the senator's farms as the senator's friends make their way to the farm where the Achaean/Greeks are to stay.

The Troas signposts, pointing to where they are to stay, are for those acting as Phrygians, Lycians, Thracians and Trojans.

Julia explains, 'All Troas will be dressed in black as well as the farm workers on that side of the river. The farm workers will not be wearing head gear, so it will be easy to identify them should you require information on where to go.

'Thracians, Lycians and Phrygians they will all be wearing caps with the pointed peak resting towards their forehead or helmets. Apart from friends who I have invited, says, Julia, all other roles are mainly taken students, who will also be carrying weapons.'

Marcus and Petrus walk towards the farm on the left-hand side of the river, and notice that not only was there a large farmhouse, but also smaller housing, cottages and barns.

They find the bedroom where they will be sleeping, and on Marcus' bed is placed black clothing, black wig, helmet, spears and shield.

There is a notice telling them to stay on the Trojan side of the river, unless they are taking part in any fighting scenes.

Marcus holds up his black wig, which has been provided for all the Trojans, and noticed that on the other side of the river the Achaean/Greeks were wearing white clothing and blonde wigs. Well at least they would be able to tell whom they are fighting against when in battle.

Although he is sharing a room with Petrus, they will be dressing differently.

Dressing as the god *Apollo*, Petrus will be wearing white clothing. *Apollo* has a laurel wreath around his head and carries a lyre, as the god is known for his music

A short while later he sees *Artemis* the twin sister of *Apollo,* is being acted by Lucy, who has bows and arrows. Both are on the side of the

Trojans. All the gods are wearing blonde wigs and white clothing.

Marcus, dresses himself as *Hector* – the son of king *Priam*, puts on a black tunic, then places his greaves onto his shins and fixes them in place with clasps.

He decides that the helmet with two oval shaped holes for the eyes and an elongated piece to cover his nose makes it was hard to see people on the left of the right without turning his head, and also not so easy to hear people speak because the helmet has a flap to protect the ears, which can block some of the sound. He decides to place it on his head at the last minute. His name is on his helmet and on the back of his clothing, like all other warriors.

He knows that in the story his character, *Hector,* is viciously killed by *Achilles*. He wonders which of the senator's friends will be taking on the role of *Achilles*. He decides to look out for anyone walking around with the name on his helmet, hoping that the vicious bit was only in the story and not going to happen in the war game.

Other men playing the Trojans also wondered whom they will be fighting against, and are particularly looking out for the names *Menelaus*, *Odysseus* and especially *Diomedes*.

'From what I understand, the senator and his friends take this war game quite seriously, but I don't think they exactly follow the story because there are not enough people and very little time. We will just enjoy it as a game,' says Marcus hoping that he does not walk away with too many injuries.

Besides Petrus and the goddess *Artemis*, there is another goddess, *Aphrodite*, known to the Romans as *Venus*, and the god *Ares,* whom the Romans called *Mars*. Honey-Bee is to play *Aphrodite* and Rufus the god *Ares*.

Papinus came up to them saying, 'Anyone injured will be given a red spot to show where the injury is, such as arm, chest, leg and so on. There are organisers who will tell you whether you are out of the fight, or to continue. They know the story better than most people taking part.

'A notice board, down by the river, provides an explanation, with maps, and where the scenes are taking place.

'Should you feel the cold, you may wear trousers under your tunics, and even a cloak, but bear in mind that those fighting near the river could possibly get their clothes wet, so don't wear trousers unless absolutely necessary.

'There is not enough time, during a weekend, to carry out every part of Homer's *'The Iliad'* story – so just count it as a game, the weapons are not dangerous, and the game and not an exact account of the whole Trojan War.'

'We do not have hundreds of Achaean/Greek ships, so in the widest part of the river, which is only waist height, there were a few boats usually for fishing – you will have to use your imagination when the fighting takes place at that point.

'The war game will begin at 12.00 mid-day. Enjoy you weekend.'

*

Walking around they discover where to eat, drink, bathe, and where guests are housed.

Lycus says to Marcus. 'Honey-Bee and I only arrived from Capri yesterday.'

'I'm pleased to see you – acting as *Paris*,' replies Marcus.

'Yes, I so looking forward to it.'

'Honey-Bee will be acting as *Aphrodite*, in other words the beautiful Roman *Venus*.'

'Oh, she'll love that part.'

Lycus asks, 'So who is playing the role of *Helen* of Troy?'

'See the red-haired woman walking towards us – well that is Anna.'

'Wow – I don't mind being locked away in the palace with her – I think the story says that *Helen* of Troy and *Paris* have to spend most of their time together?'

'Yes, but you do have some acting roles and a bit of fighting as well.'

'Quickly, we must finish putting on our outfits because it is nearly time for the games to begin.'

'Honey-Bee, when you have changed, you must make your way towards the bridge across the river where you will see Petrus, who is the god *Apollo*.'

Petrus is joined by Rufus, acting as *Ares,* the god of war.

Lucy changes into her costume as the goddess, *Artemis*, and walks down to the bridge by the river where Honey-bee, and the Trojan gods and goddesses are positioned on the Trojan end of the bridge.

On the other side of the bridge sit the Achaean/Greeks gods and goddesses. Their faces were not familiar to Honey-Bee or Lucy.

Positioned in the middle of the bridge is *Zeus*, who is supposed to be neutral.

The gods and goddesses for the Achaean/Greeks look across at the Trojans as they begin to take their seats to view the battle.

The Achaean/Greek gods and goddesses, are *Hera* the wife of *Zeus*, and *Athena*. Both women wish to destroy Troy. *Zeus* wants to choose his moment when this will happen, but tries to remain neutral.

The two Achaean/Greek gods positioned by the bridge with the other gods, are *Poseidon* who had helped to build the walls of Troy some time back and felt that he had not been recompensed, so in Homer's story he is not exactly sympathetically drawn towards the Trojans.

The other god is *Hephaestus* had been slighted, because the Trojan god *Ares,* had previously had an affair with the Trojan goddess *Aphrodite* who was *Hephaestus*' wife. Hephaestus makes the weapons for the Achaean/Greeks and this does not bode well for the gods and goddesses who support the Trojans, such as *Apollo, Artemis, Ares*, and *Aphrodite*.

Sextus is now dressed as the Trojan king, *Priam*. Sextus does not have too much acting to do, but this suits him – a small role give him an excuse to join in the weekend game.

The 'Troas', secretly decide that in the evening they will make an undercover raiding party into the Achaean/Greeks' camp to see if they are receiving better food, wine, blankets and pillows. They will bring back food and wine to the Troas camp, but return any plates, glasses the following day and leave a sign saying that they have raided the opposition's camp.

Honey-Bee asks, 'Who are the Achaeans and the Trojans?'

Papinus replies: 'The Achaean/Greeks are the ancient people who lived either in Greece or on the Greek islands. The Trojans were people of Asia-Minor – being lands between the Hellespont, Bosporus, the Mediterranean and the Black Sea, and across into parts of Europe.

'Across, by ship, the other side of the Hellespont is Europe where the Thracians live, and are supporters. The Hellespont leads into the Aegean Sea, and in the opposite direction is the Propontis and the Bosphorus to the Black Sea.'

'Who are the Phrygians?'

'They were closely connected to the Trojans in Asia Minor, as the Trojan king *Priam*'s wife is

Phrygian. Close to the Hellespont, the Trojans have a natural harbour which also protects their land.'

Lucy asked: 'Do you think that the ancient Greeks, who were sea going people, wanted to travel in their ships from the Mediterranean and through the Hellespont to the Black Sea, perhaps for trading purposes?'

'We are not concerned with the initial reasons for the long war – only the story as told by Homer, relating to the rage of *Achilles* and *Helen* of Troy and not with the fall of Troy nor the Trojan horse.'

Those around him looked a little puzzled because they expected the story of the Trojan horse that was sent into Troy to be part of the story.

Papinus replies to Lucy. 'The story of the fall of Troy is not in Homer's story of the *Iliad*. The fall of Troy comes under Homer's other story the *Odyssey*. Not factual, but it provides an insight into the ancient Bronze and Iron Age world. We can learn about their warfare, their sense of honour, and how the people unite and support each other – Greeks and their island peoples who rely on the sea.

'It is similar for the peoples of Asia Minor having similar principles, who rely on the land for their horses and trading for their survival.

'In the *Iliad,* the story by Homer shows how human conflicts, emotions, and how decisions are made. Kings, commanders, and leaders, honour their agreements, and place their lives, their country, and fighting men above that of their own lives. Their lives are for their community, honouring and giving respect for age-old traditions.

'The ancient gods and goddesses do not experience death. Injuries are healed, and they do not suffer hardship like humans, or experience the pain of losing a loved.

'All of you taking part, will realise at the end of the weekend that your own characters, friendships, fun and laughter will develop into strong friendships. A story, within a story. Please enjoy the weekend.'

*

Everyone looks at the notice board to find where he or she should be placed on the battlefield.

In the middle of the bridge sits *Zeus,* in his supposed neutral position. Petrus and Marcus immediately recognise Crispus in the role of *Zeus*.

Marcus remembered that Crispus' wife, being of an old aristocratic family, probably allows Crispus to get a role in this key position. Aristocrats with names going back to ancient times are largely disappearing, but are proud to show themselves as landowners of large tracks of land in Italy.

Marcus greets Crispus, and asked if his wife is attending. 'No,' he replies.

The Troas agreed that *Zeus* was supposed to be neutral - but can we trust Crispus to act kindly towards the friends acting as Trojans.

Petrus explains to the rest of the Trojan team about selling a house that Crispus had desired, but then his wife beat him on the deal, making her the sole owner.

Papinus came up with an idea. 'We shall send a messenger, to make haste to Crispus' wife, asking her to join us and play the part of *Hector*'s wife. We will send her the correct clothing, so that no time is wasted.'

They all thought that it would stop Crispus from over-playing his role. When he sees his wife on the

Trojan team and appearing in the role of *Hector*'s wife, perhaps he would soften a little.

Neither Papinus nor Lucy is happy to see Messalina as *Hera*.

On the furthest side of *Hera* sits the goddess *Athena* and the two Achaean/Greek gods, *Poseidon* and *Hephaestus*. The Troas do not recognise the faces of these people, especially when they are all in white, as well as wearing white wigs and helmets.

The senator's friends who had attended all previous war games take their usual positions, by the ships or the campsite, ready for battle. As the Troas looked across at their camp they can see *Odysseus* glaring back at them.

The Trojans were beginning to gather close to the grounds in front of the farmhouse, (which has temporarily become the Trojan palace), and the sloping land down to the river.

'I remember', said Marcus looking at his armour, 'that when seeing the pottery figures in Julia's shop, ancient Achaean/Greeks are holding shields in their left hand. On the inside of the shields there are supports for the elbow and on the inside edge can be seen a handgrip'.

The Troas looked at their own shields, which the senator had provided for them. They were disappointed to find that their shields were only supported on the body by a leather strap.

'Do you think the senator has made a mistake?' asked Rufus.

Papinus replies, 'The leather support strap is called a 'baldric' and ancient warriors such as the Thracians and Phrygians, and other tribes who were horse warriors, could wear their shields on their backs whilst riding,'

'Tough on me', laughs Rufus, 'it takes me all my time to sit on a horse and turn backwards whilst the horse is trotting, let alone shoot backwards at the same time.'

'They also have short swords on the baldric or a scabbard. Of course, the Troas on this occasion have only been supplied with soft-wooden weapons, or those made of skin or other soft materials,' says Papinus.

'Well I suppose we had better get in a bit of practice holding all these things – otherwise I can do myself some serious injury,' jokes Marcus.

On the way towards the river, they pass encampments of those students who are acting as tribal people on the Trojan side. One group are

Phrygian. In the story king *Priam*'s wife is Phrygian.

Some people in the group wear soft leather fitted peak caps, with a point at the top coming down towards the forehead. But others wear similar caps but the leather has a coating of bronze, and flaps covering their ears. One group have arrows and bended bows.

Tribes represented were in camps either situated down near the water or further up towards the so-called citadel, being the farmhouse where the Troas are based. Others are mid-ground.

Arriving only just in time are the Thracians, who are on the side of the Trojans.

Keeping with Homer's *Iliad* story, they arrive late at the camp. King *Rhesus*, has his silver chariot with white horses and his soldiers in full gear arriving on their horses. They do not join everyone by the bridge or river.

The men decide to rest sleeping close by their horses. According to Homer's story, they had been delayed due to fighting with the Scythians who, like the Phrygians, also had their homeland in Eastern Europe.

Out of the corner of his eye Rufus notices that the Thracians have positioned a Draco wolf or dragon head at each corner where they are camped. Should the wind blow the body of the Draco, will move about and should frighten intruders and also awaken the resting soldiers. Lucy had previously told him of her meeting with Messalina and the dragon jumping out at the door.

The warriors are wearing soft boots that cover their ankles, long loose fitting trousers from the waist to their boots, and long tunics that came down to the calves of their legs, and over that their cloaks held together with a clasp on the right shoulder. Their clothing was very suitable for warriors on horseback. They have spears close by their sides, and a large curved dagger or curved sword, a *falax*, and rest with their weapons placed next to them.

*

Saturday afternoon – the Story of Helen

Papinus gathers them all around and tells them, how *Helen* was taken off to Troy, by *Paris*.

'*Helen* and *Clytemnestra* were sisters. *Clytemnestra* was the wife of king *Agamemnon*, king of Mycenae. He was the commander of all the warriors, Achaean/Greeks, who were fighting against the Trojans in a war that had carried on for over nine years. His brother. *Menelaus*, was a king of Sparta, in the earlier years of Spartan history.

'*Helen* was very beautiful, and had many suitors for her hand in marriage. The suitors agree a pact – whichever of the suitors she should choose – nobody else should attempt to break up the marriage. King *Menelaus* was chosen by *Helen* to be her husband.

'The tale of *Helen* of Troy and *Paris* began with an apple. There was a wedding at which the goddess of *Discord*, who had not been invited, threw an apple to whoever is chosen the most fairest goddess. This caused strife when *Zeus*' wife, the goddess *Hera* and the goddess *Athena,* thought they were the most beautiful. *Aphrodite,* the beautiful goddess of love, did not wish to be chosen.

'*Zeus* told the god *Hermes* to get the mortal *Paris,* who was a wedding guest, to make the choice. *Paris,* now under godly influence, saw *Helen* as the most beautiful and immediately fell in love with her. Returning home to Troy, with the wife of king *Menelaus.*

'The two kings of Mycenae Sparta and Mycenae Argos, *Menelaus* and *Agamemnon,* called up the warriors, especially *Achilles* and cousin *Ajax* to help in the fight to return *Helen*.

'They receive support from many kings and warriors of Achaean/Greek lands, being those on the east of the Ionian Sea and west of the Aegean Sea and islands such as Crete, and their catalogue of ships, to fight for the return of *Helen*.

'The Trojan *Paris* refuses the request to return *Helen* to *Menelaus*. However, within the Achaean/Greek camp a separate situation has arisen between king *Agamemnon* and the warrior, *Achilles*.

'In an earlier fight between the Achaean/Greeks and the Trojans, king *Agamemnon* has returned to camp with his trophy from Troy, being the capture of *Chryseis,* the daughter of a priest of *Zeus*. The priest appealed to *Zeus* for the return of his daughter.

'King *Agamemnon* is told to return *Chryseis,* but when he refuses, the god *Apollo,* who is on the Trojan side, sends arrows causing damage to the Achaean/Greek soldiers and affecting them with a plague.

'Eventually, *Odysseus,* a leading warrior on the Achaean/Greeks side, persuades *Agamemnon* to return *Chryseis.*

'However, it is normal practice after winning a battle, for the main warrior or commander to receive honour from his soldiers by receiving the most prized war trophy. This must be better than any other trophies retrieved from the battleground.

'King *Agamemnon* is not going to easily give up his trophy and lose face. He demands that *Achilles* the warrior, but not king or chief of the forces, forfeit his own trophy to Agamemnon. *Achilles*' prize is a Trojan captive named *Briseis,* a woman to whom he has grown quite fond.

'*Achilles*, also not wanting to lose face with his own warriors, strongly objects, but is forced to forfeit his prize, and stubbornly refuses to fight any further. This action which he has chosen, will causes great loss of life on the battlefield.'

The Troas are now aware of their roles in the game, which is about to start.

*

War begins with a sulk

The scene begins on the Achaean/Greek side of the river, with trouble amongst themselves.

The priest of *Apollo* (acted by Petrus) requests the return of his daughter who had been captured as trophy by *Agamemnon* (played by Dio, the senator's friend). He returns the daughter but takes *Achilles* trophy *Briseis*. *Achilles* (played by Julia's father) captured her from the previous battle against the Trojans – but was now being forced to hand her over to *Agamemnon,* which in the eyes of his soldiers places him as a leader without a trophy. He retaliates by refusing to join his commander in battle against the Trojans, and sits in his tent in a huff.

Julia's father is not noticed in his tent, acting as *Achilles*. Marcus has been wandering around talking to people and trying in search of someone with the name *Achilles* written on the back of his clothing.

Thetis, a sea nymph and mother of *Achilles*, goes to *Zeus* (acted by Crispus) – suggesting that if the Trojans can win a small victory in battle, then this may bring her son into action to join his comrades and fight against the Trojans – rather than see his own side lose. *Zeus* is interested, but *Hera,* (play by Messalina), being *Zeus*' wife, raises her objections.

Zeus gives a dream to *Agamemnon* that the Trojans will win if there were a battle. *Agamemnon* puts his men into action, but *Zeus* counteracts this by getting *Agamemnon*'s men fall back, possibly created an idea that the Greeks are losing the fight and that *Achilles* will jump up and act – a win/lose situation.

Odysseus, son of a king, encourages the men by getting the Achaean/Greeks to reassemble for action near their ships. On no account must they lose their ships because they need them to return to their homelands.

It is agreed by both sides, to avoid loss of many warriors, that it is wiser for a duel to take place, where the winner takes *Helen* of Troy. *Paris* is reluctant to fight, but his father, *Priam*, and brother, *Hector*, tell him that he must take part.

But Lycus (in the role of *Paris*) has not been expecting to take part in a duel. He had understood that all he needed to do was to lie in bed for his part in the game, in the palace of Troy with the beautiful *Helen* (the red-haired Anna).

Menelaus, the king of Sparta, who has the support of many ships and many warriors, is prepared to fight *Paris* for the return of his wife.

Looking across at the man, Lycus wonders whether he stands a chance – the man in the role as *Menelaus* looks like a man who is a commander of Roman legions and now, possibly a senator. Everything about him looks military.

Lycus cannot get out of the role of playing *Paris*, but feels like shouting out to *Menelaus* that he is part Greek by birth, and should be fighting on the Achaean/Greek side. But he realises that every one of the Troas are friends and they are expecting him to take on the challenge.

In Homer's story, *Paris,* even though nervous about fighting *Menelaus,* has no intention of returning *Helen* to her husband.

Earlier Lycus had wrapped his greaves around his legs for protection. These were held together with clasps made of silver, then he donned his breastplate, his bronze sword was hanging from his shoulder, then the strap for his shield, and his helmet made by the blacksmith with cheek covers.

Horsehair atop his helmet tosses about as he walks, and in the sunlight bristles and it even frightens himself when he sees his shadow contrasting fiercely against the sunlight.

Their armies stand with their weapons and shields at their sides, and lances planted upright in the soil, which they lean upon and wait for the duel to begin.

Lycus, bravely acting as *Paris*, stands facing *Menelaus*. Both men are across from each other, their bronze armour gleaming, and prepared for battle.

Paris has a moment of feeling cowardly but *Hector* (played by Marcus) snaps him out of it.

The two warriors, as Homer imagines the fight, choose their rugged spears. *Menelaus* is victorious and all the Achaean/Greeks on the senator's side are cheering on their man.

Paris hurls his spear – its point slightly bends as it hits the centre of the opponent's shield. *Menelaus* hurls his spear but, just as it is about hit Paris' breastplate, *Paris* turns his body, and is not severely injured. Quickly *Menelaus* uses his sword to smash *Paris*'s helmet but his sword gets damaged.

Menelaus then takes hold of the horsehair atop *Paris*'s helmet, swinging his prey as he drags him towards the lines of the Achaeans/Greeks. The strap of the helmet is cutting into *Paris*' throat and he is being strangled.

Lycus – who is fighting to breath, especially after having his breastplate hit – fortunately manages to move his body slightly. But now *Menelaus* is really strangling him. *Menelaus* is pulling at his headgear and nearly breaking the strap and ready to hit him with a spear – at that very moment Lycus is feeling that he should just walk away from the so-called game.

But Homer, the ancient storyteller, in order to save *Paris*, allows the Trojan goddess, *Aphrodite* (who is Honey-Bee), to cut the leather strap. *Menelaus* throws the helmet towards his bystanders.

Paris has not given up, but just as *Menelaus* brings out his spear, the goddess, *Aphrodite,* uses her powers to sweep *Paris* away in a mist of clouds (which the organizers of the event had made from soft boards) and placed him safely within the Trojan walls.

The goddess, *Aphrodite,* was somehow one of the conspirators who caused *Paris* to fall in love with *Helen of Troy*, so felt a responsibility to save the Trojan.

The departure of Paris from the contest does not bring the war to a conclusion. *Menelaus* is considered the winner – Paris had reneged on the deal by being the loser and has not returned *Helen.*

*

Suddenly *Helen* in the form of red-haired Anna appears at Lycus' side. He now felt that after all the trauma, there was a turn-around and things were starting to look upward.

His neck was sore after nearly being strangulated – fortunately the strap was made of soft leather. The shield had protected his body, but he has slight difficulty when breathing, after being hit in the chest. But upon meeting Anna his pain temporarily disappears.

He does not want to remove his cuirass (breastplate) just in case he is called to fight again, and he needs his body protected. It took so long to get this equipment on with all the tying and buckling. Much better being a sailor at sea, even if one is at risk from pirates.

They decide to take a walk and arrive at the barn. Anna helps him up the ladder to the platform that holds the soft straw. Telling him to lie down and recover from his fight, and finds a little water and a cloth.

Upon returning she gently wipes his neck. She is so close that he gets an urge to kiss her, but holds back. He becomes entranced with her pale white skin and red hair and wants to touch it.

Then realises that his neck is painful when he lifts his head.

He was somewhat disappointed that he did not have the injury 'red spots' given to him. Others who were injured had stickers placed on them to show the rest of the people in the war game where they had been injured. Then he remembers how *Aphrodite* quickly whisked him away. Better than being left in the hands of king *Menelaus*. Goodness knows what fate would have awaited him!

Anna asks him about his chest – after being hit by *Menelaus*' spear. 'I will see if I can rub your chest. But first let me gently wipe you neck with this cool water.'

A few travelling musicians and dancers, who are to entertain everyone in the evening, practise outside the barn. The music is quite melodic and soothing.

It was difficult to reach his chest as he still has on all his armour, ready to take part in the fighting and there were straps on the shoulders.

Anna sat astride his legs, avoiding the greaves and the breastplate. She told him to lie flat and she would move her hands beneath the armour. Her hand moves under the lower part of the breastplate, which can only happen if he breathes in deeply.

This action hurt him – but he enjoys having her gentle hands roaming around trying to find the spot that is injured or feeling very sore.

Her palms reached up to the sore spot in time to the rhythm of the music, breathing in and out. Now he begins to find this feeling unimaginable – a mixture between gentle caress to his aching body and the contrasting experience of being strapped to his body armour. In his mind he wants to bring his hands up to rub the sides of her body – but the pain from the spear hitting his body shield had left him bruised.

Suddenly, not far away Lycus can hear Honey-Bee calling his name. Anna slithers out her hand and he reluctantly stands up to leave.

He hastily gives Anna a quick parting kiss of thanks. His aches and pains are returning as he moves down the platform ladder, collecting the rest of his weaponry and, swift-footed, Lycus climbs out through a side window, to prevent Honey-Bee entering the barn.

Anna could hear him explaining to Honey-Bee that he was some distance away when he heard her calling his name. He convinces himself that he was some distance away – both in presence and emotion.

'The fight must have given you a shock – and disappointment,' said Honey-Bee.

'Oh, everything improved when I lay back – I really needed a longer recovering time', remarks Lycus, yet wishing he could be back in the barn being rubbed.

Anna smiles to herself as she makes her way out of the barn. She had stopped acting out her role as the goddess. She used to take part in small plays along with her friends when in England. She found it fun to tease Lycus.

*

Colliding gods like invisible atoms

Paris' vanishing act, was brought into effect by the Trojan goddess *Aphrodite*. Homer begins to inspire the interest of the other gods with intrusions and intrigues. The Achaean/Greek goddesses and gods use their own nefarious tit-for-tat acts against the Trojan gods and humans.

The Achaean/Greek goddess, *Athena*, disguises herself as the Trojan warrior *Pandarus,* (acted by Fabius) known as being an excellent marksman with arrows. *Athena-cum-imaginary Pandarus* shoots an arrow at the Spartan king, *Menelaus*. The intention is not to kill *Menelaus*, but just to wound him, and cause anger. *Athena* then uses her powers to deflect the arrow on the last minute, only causing slight injuries.

The warriors on the Achaean/Greek side, *Odysseus, Diomedes,* and *Agamemnon* rally their men. The senator's friend, the consul, is acting as *Diomedes*.

Neither the Achaean/Greeks nor the Trojans, approve of *Paris'* behaviour. The situation can only be solved if he returns *Helen* to *Menelaus*. The latter has been the winner of the duel.

*

Oscillating between gods and goddesses

Pandarus, having supposedly injured *Menelaus* (with the cunning of goddess Athena in the guise of Pandarus) also slightly injures *Diomedes* to encourage him to fight the Trojans.

The goddess *Athena*, now strengthens *Diomedes* (acted by the consul) to become the best warrior, by providing him with a helmet that can spurt out fire, and having a special visor that allows him to differentiate between humans and gods when he is fighting.

Diomedes wounds the Trojan *Aeneas*, but his mother *Aphrodite* comes to his rescue. *Diomedes,* with his special glasses, is not supposed to injure gods and goddesses, yet manages to inflict a cut on *Aphrodite*'s wrist.

Zeus tells *Aphrodite* that she should not become involved in the war. The Trojan goddess had already whisked away *Paris*, which had caused both sides of the gods to take action.

Apollo, a Trojan god, (played by Petrus) now becomes involved, and provides assistance to *Aeneas*. *Aeneas* cannot be allowed to die because he makes an appearance in Homer's next story – and also a later story by the Roman writer Virgil in his book *Aeneid.*

The god, *Apollo,* uses his special powers to leave a replica of *Aeneas* to encourage the Trojans to continue fighting with zest so that they have the belief that he is fighting alongside the men.

Diomedes who is wearing his special visor, manages to attack *Apollo*. But he has been told not to attack the gods and the special visor is supposed to differentiate gods from man.

The goddess *Athena,* who enjoys getting involved in the war, decides to battle with the god *Ares* (who is played by Rufus).

Hera and *Athena*, seek permission from *Zeus* to encourage the Achaean/Greeks to win the battle.

Athena tells the invincible *Diomedes* that he can attack the god *Ares* and she rides with him to chase after *Ares*. *Ares* only has *Diomedes* in his sight; he cannot see *Athena* because she is wearing a special helmet to make her invisible. *Diomedes* shoots an arrow; which *Athena* directs to *Ares* shoulder. It is now a battle between the Achaean/Greek goddess *Athena*, and Trojan god, *Ares*.

Ares complains, but *Zeus* gives no sympathy. *Ares* injury is not going to have an effect on *Zeus'* grand plan to get *Achilles* to join the battle and bring down Troy.

Hector (played by Marcus) knows that his fate is close at hand, he speaks with his wife *Andromache*, (who is being acted by Crispus' wife). *Hector* takes off his helmet, with horsehair that bristles, so that his son can see his face and not be frightened with his father wearing a helmet. It is an act of human compassion for his family at a time of war. She offers him the libation cup consisting of a mixture of wine, honey and water.

A little offering is given to *Zeus* and the gods, and a little on the ground for those that have died, some for *Hector* to drink and those around him. *Andromache* leads the women in prayer at the altar for *Athena* with the hope for her family and the Trojans.

Whilst this is going on Crispus, who is in the role of *Zeus*, is somewhat disturbed when seeing his wife on the side of the Trojans, and acting as the wife of *Hector*.

Hector now takes part in the fight, but then it is decided that there should be a dual. *Hector* is to dual with one of the Achaean/Greeks.

The Achaean/Greek warriors are all offering to take part. *Ajax* a leading warrior is chosen. After tossing spears and lances, *Ajax* slightly wounds *Hector*.

As they begin to fight with swords, it was decided by the Achaean/Greeks that the night was setting in, and they request time to pay tribute to the dead and burials. King *Priam*, a role played by Sextus, agrees that the Trojans need to do the same for their dead.

After calling off the duel, *Hector* and *Ajax* show their honour by exchanging gifts, as is the custom.

King *Priam* asks his advisor to speak with *Paris* to return *Helen* to *Menelaus* so that the fighting may cease. Should the Trojans lose the war, the families, homes, and city would be lost forever.

*

Searching for one's other half

Meanwhile, Honey-bee, has not been able move from her position by the bridge, acting as the goddess *Aphrodite,* and wants to find out what Lycus is up to with Anna, who is very attractive.

Honey-Bee does not really understand all the actions taking place in the Trojan War, as she remembers little of the story. She wonders why *Paris* refuses to return *Helen*. Perhaps Lycus has fallen in love with the red-haired woman.

Honey-bee just hopes that the Trojans or the Achaean/Greeks will quickly win and then she can go and find her husband. She does not understand that the war will continue because *Paris* refuses to return *Helen*.

Nestor suggests building fortifications to protect their Achaean/Greek ships and camp.

Peace talks have taken place and the Trojans are prepared to hand over *Helen,* but *Paris* still refuses. He offers to return trophy that he had acquired at the time of taking *Helen*, but will not agree to return *Helen* to her husband *Menelaus.*

Zeus looks at the Trojan landscape and realises that the Achaean/Greeks are on lower ground. In order to move the battle along, he brings lightning and heavy showers, which causes the soldiers to run for cover. *Zeus* does not want the war to end until *Achilles* joins the fight.

Hector sees the elderly *Nestor* without support of his Achaean/Greek soldiers. *Hector* charges forth, but *Diomedes* picks up *Nestor* in his chariot. The Trojans chase after them until they reach the fortifications.

The fortifications around the Achaean/Greek camp prevented *Hector* from entering the area, but he decides on a plan that can be set in motion - to set fire to their ships.

The Achaean/Greeks are seafaring people and each island, or area, owns many ships for their livelihood and survival. Most of them are in the waters close to Troy. The burning of their ships will cause great losses.

With a plan in mind, *Hector* tells his men to camp outside the walls of Troy and to light camp fires.

Agamemnon is disappointed that they have been driven back and *Nestor* suggests the Achaean/Greeks make amends with *Achilles* and offer him gifts of persuasion. They find him in his tent with *Patroclus*, who is his close childhood friend, playing music on a lyre. He contemplates about whether he should return to live in peace with his father, a king – or be heroic, yet knowing his life will not be long nor peaceful.

Achilles makes the decision to remain in his tent near the ships and await the threat of the arrival of the Trojans.

Nestor decides on a night-time reconnaissance into the Trojan territory. D*iomedes* and *Odysseus* volunteer, praying beforehand for *Athena*'s protection and victory.

At the same time, in the opposite direction, *Hector* decides to send the Trojan *Dolon*, (Papinus in this role) on a similar mission. *Hector* promises *Dolon* that if he succeeds in his mission to find out information on the positioning of the Achaean/Greek warriors in their camp and by their ships, then *Dolon* will be rewarded with the trophy of *Achilles'* horses and chariot.

Achilles' horses had been given to him by his father Peleus. Peleus had received two immortal horses from *Poseidon* as a wedding gift. *Achilles* had also added a mortal horse called Pedesos as the trace horse. The horses are much loved, and *Patroclus*, *Achilles'* closest friend, feeds them every day.

This is an outstanding reward for *Dolon*, yet at the same time, this is a mission which he has to undertake with no support.

Unfortunately, *Dolon* is captured by *Diomedes* and *Odysseus* and he is forced to reveal the Trojan positions. He also tells them that the Thracians are allies and are at their camp. The Thracians are asleep under the stars, with their horses, and have covered themselves with blankets.

Diomedes then kills *Dolon* and takes his armour. They proceed undercover to the Trojan camp and find the Thracians sleeping after an exhausting journey and fighting the previous days with the Scythians.

Diomedes and *Odysseus* kill the Thracians and King *Rhesus* and take the king's chariot and horses.

The very same evening when *Diomedes*, *Odysseus* are inside the Trojan boundary killing *Dolon* and the Thracians, the Roman Troas, consisting of Marcus, Rufus, Fabius and Petrus decide to make their secret raid on the Achaean/Greek camp, on the opposite side of the small river. Their mission is just for fun and to bring back any pies, cakes, goodies, and trophies of glasses or mugs, which they will return on Sunday evening at the main closing event.

It is the Roman custom for hosts to serve poorer quality food to people of a lower status. This makes them decide to bring back some wine and check if there is a difference to what the senator's friends are eating and drinking.

They colour their cheeks with Lucy's black mascara, so that their faces will not shine in the moonlight, and borrow Phrygian caps to cover their heads. The Trojan clothing is black, so little disguise is needed.

They take with them their imitation soft wooden Trojan weapons, and Lucy's red nail polish to make their mark when inside the Achaean/Greek camp indicating their accomplished raid.

But before departure, they clasp shoulders together and quietly say: 'All for one – if anyone takes one of us hostage, we will all join in the rescue.'

They disappear down to the river. When drawing close to the opposite side of the river, they notice some Achaean/Greeks are guarding the area, even though the war games had stopped for the night. They creep on all fours up the bank to the tents.

Several people are still drinking and talking. A few servants sit in a huddle a little further away eating and talking.

The Troas have taken pillowcases from their own camp and begin filling these with pies, biscuits and cakes. Others quietly put tableware close to their bodies to prevent them from making a noise. Marcus finds a small amphora of wine on a table – he lifts this up. It is half full.

As they make ready to return to their own camp, a few men dressed as Achaean/Greeks come outside a tent where they had been drinking. They place a large silver bowl on the ground and begin playing a game to see who can urinate inside the bowl ... laughing and jeering at those who miss.

One man slightly misses the target is dressed as *Achilles*. All the so-called Achaean/Greek friends who are present, chase him, laughing as they run and throwing cakes at each other.

But Marcus' attention is drawn towards a woman in the distance, dressed as *Athena*, she is talking to someone. He is shocked to see that *Athena* is Julia. She had not told him that she would be on the opposing side, and he had forgotten to ask her which part she would be playing in the war game.

Rufus quietly tips out the urine, gives the bowl a wash from a trough nearby, and takes the bowl and places it on top of one of the empty tents, for them to discover in the morning – and circling an area around it with the red nail varnish.

On their way back to the Trojan side, Marcus says to Petrus, 'I noticed that Crispus (*Zeus*) did not seem part of the group, and the man dressed as *Achilles* who they threw cakes at looks rather familiar.

'Oh, *Achilles* is Julia's father, Quintus the senator. Lucy told me that he was taking that role.

'Then if I am in the role of *Hector*, and the senator is *Achilles*, then he will be attacking me!'

'He is probably going to put you to the test to see if you are suitable for his daughter.'

The Troas took their trophy of food and wine, along with the items that were to be returned the following day – creeping quietly in the still night, back to their own camp.

In the morning there was lots of hustle and bustle as people wash, dress and eat.

It seems that Marcus and friends were not the only ones who were crossing to the other camp that night. Their trip was for fun – but it was a shock for Marcus to see Julia on the opposing side, and her father wishing to fight him.

CHAPTER ELEVEN

Sunday Game – Construing the Trojan War

It is now Sunday, the last day. The last day for the Trojan War, and a long day as they will fight until sunset.

It was not until the morning when they learn that the Achaean/Greeks, *Diomedes* and *Odysseus*, had supposedly killed *Dolon,* as well as the Thracians and taken the king's possessions, during the night.

Word came down from the battlefield informing *Hector* that one of the Trojan warriors has managed to injure *Agamemnon*, and the kings pain forces him to leave the fight.

As the fighting continues, *Diomedes* and *Odysseus* are injured.

But *Diomedes* does not stay away for long. Upon his return to the battle he hurls a spear when *Hector* charges a line of warriors. *Diomedes'* spear damages *Hector*'s helmet, and he moves back.

Paris now gets in on the action and wounds *Diomedes* with an arrow.

Odysseus, who has also returned to the fight, finds himself encircled by the Trojans and is wounded through the ribs, but is rescued by one of his supporting warriors.

The Achaeans/Greeks are preparing to save their ships. The Trojans have shattered a defence gate with a boulder, which leaves the camp vulnerable to attack. The Achaeans/Greeks are now aware that the Trojans are planning the put fire to the ships.

Zeus knows that Troy will fall, and hopes at this point of the war that *Achilles* will join in the battle for victory.

Achilles still refuses to help.

His very close boyhood friend *Patroclus* finds it hard to watch the Achaeans/Greeks being attacked by the Trojans. He appeals to *Achilles* to let him use his special armour, which includes a shield made of several metals, as he believes that the soldiers, upon seeing the armour, will believe that *Achilles* has now joined the fight, and provide some encouragement to the men and bring fear to the Trojans.

There is still concern for their ships, and *Poseidon* gives his support to save them. Two of the Achaean/Greek warriors fight to drive back *Hector*'s men. *Hector* is supported by *Paris* and *Aeneas* (acted by Fabius). But they are now fighting within the Achaean/Greek stronghold and are being attacked on all sides.

During the battle, *Poseidon*'s grandson gets killed. And many other men on the Achaean/Greek side witness relatives and grandsons killed. Fathers and sons are all fighting, as the Trojans storm towards the ships to set fire on whose Achaean-beaked shaped vessels.

Their commanders encouraged them to fight hand-to-hand to save their ships.

Likewise, the Trojans and Lycians, and their supporters are told to fight hand-to-hand, and make for the ships.

They are fighting at close range with battle-axes, hatchets from the ships, swords and blades.

Soon, *Hector* starts a blaze on the first ship, *Zeus* decides to stop the Trojans winning streak, which he has created.

One of the Achaean/Greek warriors is given extra power by the god *Poseidon*, and this brings about a turn less favourable to the Trojans who are forced to retreat to their own territory.

They try to regroup but find so many of their men are dead or injured.

The leader *Nestor* encourages *Agamemnon* and his men, alongside *Diomedes* and *Odysseus* and their warriors, to find the strength and courage to continue to fight.

The Achaean/Greeks see an eagle and draw the conclusion that it is a good sign.

Aphrodite, the goddess on the Trojan side, possesses a special embroidered band across her breasts that possess such 'power of seduction' that men fall in love with her. She is tricked by *Hera* into to letting her borrow it.

Hera (being played by Messalina who is enthusiastic about this role) seduces *Zeus*, (Crispus is only prepared to act as if asleep and nothing further) and after the god and goddess have their imaginary sexual encounter, which they keep secretly hidden from the other gods, and with the power of the breast band, and outside influences, eventually *Zeus* to goes into a deep slumber.

Hera takes the opportunity to collude with *Poseidon* – to act against *Zeus'* wishes, and bring about a defeat of the Trojans and victory for the Achaean/Greeks.

Hector is hit by a large stone, and his supporters take him back to Troy. Large numbers of Trojans are killed and others begin to flee.

Zeus is now awake. He prevents *Poseidon* from controlling the battlefield, because *Zeus* has planned the ending himself for the Trojan prince, *Hector*, but only after *Achilles* joins in the fight.

However, *Zeus* is given an ultimatum by the gods. If he does not let *Athena, Hera* and *Hephaestus* destroy the city there will be disharmony between *Zeus* and *Poseidon*.

All the people taking part are quite exhausted after fighting most of the morning.

*

Mid-day break back on the Farm

It is time for everyone to return to their own camp to eat, drink, and take a brief rest.

The men begin to tease Honey-bee about the embroidered breast band and where she keeps it since the item is supposed to create passion in men.

'If anyone knows where it is then I will gladly take it with me to Capri,' replies Honey-bee.

'I think we should auction the breast band if anyone finds it,' smiles Petrus.

They tease Lycus about being careful about falling into a deep sleep.

'Hate to spoil the fun,' responds Papinus, 'but I think the breast band is all in the imagination.'

'I think you are in for a rough time this afternoon, Marcus, because in your role as *Hector*, you have to fight *Achilles*. Julia's father has given himself the role of *Achilles*. He will be testing whether you are a man or a mouse.'

'Whatever happens,' replies Marcus, I had better be alive by nightfall to enjoy the feast, and hopefully flirt with his daughter!'

Papinus manages to have a private word with Anna. 'I hope you can to control *Paris*. I am a little jealous, because I would like to have you by my side, and not close to *Paris*.'

'I have had fun with Lycus – but you are my kind of man – especially when you tell me about ancient gods and constellations,' she replies and squeezes his hand.

Marcus had earlier taken off his bronze helmet to relax and chatter to people. But now it is time to put on all his protective covering, and prepares himself for the fight with *Achilles*. He slowly walks back to his position in the game.

The senator, Quintus, approaches him. 'I hope you will show your skill when playing the part of *Hector*.'

'I will do my best sir.'

'My next Trojan War party will be in two years' time – hopefully you will be married to my daughter by that time. Then you may enjoy playing a warrior on Achaean/Greek team – perhaps in the role of say *Diomedes* or *Agamemnon*.'

'I can see that I am being challenged!'

'Incidentally, I know that you shared a bed with my daughter when you stayed with my friends near Terracina. I learned that she was seen to be pregnant at the time, so they said, but bear in mind that Gundher handles most of my correspondence, sending letters and reading replies.

'By the way, you were particularly chosen to play the role of *Hector* – perform well!'

With that the senator disappeared.

Julia caught up with him, with a smile on her face, 'I noticed that my father was speaking with you – I do hope you both get along – he does think a lot of you.'

Marcus just barely managed a smile, and hurries away. He is speechless.

Patroclus after pleading with *Achilles* to allow him to wear *Achilles*' armour, finally receives permission. He believes that this will boost the Achaean/Greeks and make the Trojans afraid.

Achilles' greaves are placed onto *Patroclus*' legs and secured in place by silver clasps. Next, he wears *Achilles*' breastplate and carries his shield. He slings his sword which has a blade of bronze and a silver handle, over his shoulder. Then enjoys impersonating *Achilles*.

Patroclus places on his head the tribal boar-boned headgear, lined with leather, and along with *Achilles*' Myrmidon warriors they collect horses and chariots and depart.

Achilles had prayed to *Zeus* to drive the Trojans away from their ships, and makes another prayer to *Zeus* for *Patroclus*' safe return.

Zeus only intends to grant only the first prayer.

The god has already made a promise to let the Achaean/Greeks win the war, but *Achilles* has still not joined in the war.

He creates a wild cyclone, or storm, which causes the trenches to become soaked. Making it difficult to cross the ditches, the Trojans have been forced to leave the ships.

The storm causes them to lose their military formations, and in their retreat the trench crossings present difficulty with the storm.

Chariot horizontal bars, or yokes, snap with the poor weather conditions. With the broken shafts that had supported their chariots, they construct a barrier to keep the chariots of the Achaean/Greeks at bay.

One of the Achaean/Greek warriors is aiming for *Hector*. The headgear which *Hector* is wearing makes it difficult to see and listen for shafts or spears.

Patroclus shouts to the Myrmidons warriors to slaughter the Trojans.

With determination and strength, *Patroclus* leads his warriors, with extraordinary ability to over-ride the water soaked trenches. They crash against the Trojans - their chariots causing the

Trojan axles to brake, as they fight and kill everything and everyone in their wake.

The Trojan, *Sarpendon,* (being acted by Papinus), is *Zeus'* son. He is fighting on behalf of the Trojans and is king of Lycia in Asia Minor.

Zeus, glances around the battlefield and witnesses the sight of so many men dead, or severely injured by the mindless slaughter by *Patroclus* - who had stabbed the men in their thighs, jawbones, ears, mouths, eyes, skulls – there is corpse upon corpse.

Sarpendon manages to find the leadership skills to shout at his weary Lycians – 'Find your pride and attack.'

After considerable fighting, *Sarpendon* says, 'I will go after *Patroclus* myself, and fight this Achaean/Greek man who cuts the legs off squadrons of good brave warriors.'

He jumps into his chariot and rides until he reaches *Patroclus*, and he leaps at him, fully armed – both falling onto the ground. They fight and shout their battle cries.

Zeus knows that he has caused this battle, and also knows that he will have to let *Patroclus* win and his own son die in order to encourage *Achilles* join the fight.

Hera allows the brave Lycian to kill the mortal horse of *Achilles* being used by *Patroclus*.

Sadly, *Sarpendon* is killed by *Patroclus'* spear. The Lycian king's armour is being grabbed by both sides for personal possession.

Hera, who is not *Sarpendon*'s mother, says that *Zeus* must leave him to die – but allow his burial to be given solemn honours and *Sarpendon* a tomb that befits a king.

Both *Sarpendon* and his cousin *Glaucus*, who also died, did not waiver in their battles. They were the main warriors to break through the Achaean/Greek encampment. They honoured their promise to help the Trojans who were close neighbours, even though their connections between the Achaean/Greeks and the Lycians had been an amicable one.

Even *Diomedes* honours *Glaucus* by placing his weapon into the ground knowing that *Sarpendon* and *Glaucus* were carrying out their duty to the Trojans. But their Lycian friendship with the Achaeans/Greeks will not change.

At an earlier time in the war, *Diomedes* swopped his armour with *Glaucus*, as a show of respect in his warrior commitment. Although it was said that *Glaucus* had owned the better armour.

Patroclus had been informed by *Achilles* only to fight with the men, to prevent the ships from burning. But now *Patroclus*, wearing *Achilles'* gear, and making the Trojans believe that he was *Achilles*, is wanting to fight *Hector*.

Zeus decides to punish *Patroclus* who had now taken the fight up to the gates of Troy. *Zeus* has caused *Hector* to become afraid and temporarily taken him away from the fighting. It was not in *Zeus'* plan for *Patroclus* to end the life of *Hector* without *Achilles*.

Apollo sends a message to *Patroclus* to the effect that fate is not for him to be the man who seizes Troy.

Ignoring *Apollo's* warning, he goes after *Hector* and instead kills *Hector's* half-brother who is the chariot driver, and kills him with a stone.

Hector knows full well that, when he is eventually killed by *Achilles*, there will be a battle for his own armour. He had told his wife *Andromache* about his impending death, and the eventual fall of Troy.

The Trojan god, *Apollo* comes up behind *Patroclus* when he is in the act of trying to kill

Hector. The god manages to injure *Patroclus*, who eventually dies when struck by *Hector's* spear.

Zeus wishes the war to continue. *Athena* gives *Menelaus* the strength to remove the body of *Patroclus* from the midst of battle. He tells one of the warriors to inform *Achilles*.

Hector is ready for battle, and is wearing the armour worn by *Patroclus,* which had previously been the armour belonging to *Achilles*.

The fighting continues. *Hector* tries to keep his people close to the walls for as long as possible.

Achilles' rage has moved away from *Agamemnon.* He considers whether to have a short life, avenging the death of his loyal friend *Patroclus*.

Achilles becomes reconciled with *Agamemnon* who has returned *Briseis*.

Thetis, Achilles' mother, has asked *Hephaestus* to make new weapons for her son and a shield.

Achilles, now puts on his new armour and takes the shield specially made for him by *Hephaestus,* which shows the sun, moon and constellations, among other illustrations of historic interest. He is accompanied by his Myrmidon warriors, who were men originally from Thessaly, and rides on his immortal horse named *Xanthus*.

321

Zeus now allows the other gods and goddesses to join in the fight. *Athena* wants *Aeneas* to fight *Achilles*, but *Aeneas'* life is already destined for the future.

All the senator's guests are informed that they must soon try and bring an end to the Trojan war, so that everyone may enjoy the evening.

The gods and goddesses take their seats by the bridge.

Achilles begins his fight against the Trojans, and especially *Hector* for killing his friend *Patroclus*.

Hector stays outside the walls of Troy to await a dual with *Achilles*. His father king *Priam* pleads with him to come inside the city gates.

Achilles' spear brings *Hector* down. Before dying, *Hector* asks for a burial with his own people, but *Achilles* lets the corpse be mauled and stabbed by others. Over several days the body lies with animals trying to eat parts of the corpse, but *Apollo* stands guard. That is the story according to Homer, but as this is a Trojan party for the senator, they can *not* go to such extremes, and so spare Marcus this dreadful ending.

The rage of *Achilles* has not ceased. Even the gods find *Achilles* behaviour disrespectful. His mother *Thetis* speaks with him

Zeus sends *Hermes* at night along with king *Priam*, dressed in clothing as worn by Myrmidon soldiers, so that he can get passed the guards unnoticed and to *Achilles'* tent.

King Priam discusses with *Achilles* the relationship betwcen father and son. He appeals to *Achilles* to think how his own father has love for him, as he, *Priam,* has love for his own son Hector.

Accepting an offering that *Priam* has made to *Achilles*, they share a meal. *Achilles* allows him to leave with the *Hector's* remains. Not as friends, but accepting a code of behaviour between two leading men who wish to bring an end to war and bury their dead with honour.

Achilles who was initially filled with hubris and hurt pride. But *Zeus* had waited for the young man to understand the importance of kingly respect, a code of behaviour, and standing together with one's comrades, to fight with valour for one's people and community.

Zeus allowed for the young man to make mistakes, but virtue eventually prevailed, and he became heroic as he went into battle to save his people from further bloodshed.

The senator brings to a close, the Trojan War games, by saying that, 'Homer's story takes us into a history of people, places, and mythology.

'In our year of 221, we are left to pick out parts of Homer's the story to fit in with our weekend, and perhaps others in the future will find a little time in their lives to remember Homer and the Trojan War and keep the story to be remembered in perpetuity.

'We have little concept, belief or understanding of their lives and the difficulties they faced, in those ancient times. Besides the storyteller, Homer, we also need to remember the other writers, such as Ovid, and the Greek and Roman satirists and their truths, humour and their individual take on the world.

'But now, the bonfires have been lit, meat is being cooked, the entertainment is about to start, and the younger people have taken part in the athletics and won their prizes, we will all join together in an evening of fun.'

*

Marcus and friends, like naughty schoolboys, returned their trophy from their camp raid the previous night. They all enjoyed the joke about the silver bowl being found on top of the tent post.

Musicians, entertainers, who are travellers from the Middle East, sell their wares, and provided music. Julia buys some of their eastern perfumes and several scarves.

The senator and his friends were discussing how much money they had collected form the participants at the Trojan games, and how they would give it to their chosen orphanages. They normally contribute, but the Trojan games allowed for extra improvements. The children are from good families where a father had died or suffered from a debt problem.

Messalina wanders around looking for food she can take home with her. Crispus is tired and decides to return home. He offers to give her a ride in his carriage, as she does not wish to spend the Sunday night at the farm.

Crispus is barely listening as she tells him about how she learned to stand on her head by a wonderful man in India.

He catches her last few words and asks, 'When were you in India?'

'I was not in the country India. My wonderful friend had a house that he called "India" because he had visited the country and loved it. He brought back lots of brass and silver ornaments and always had incense burning. It was in "India" the house, where I learned the art of handstands and many other wonderful body movements for one's health.'

Crispus gives his usual humph and moves towards his carriage.

Eventually everyone is exhausted and go their various ways.

*

An End to an Exciting Weekend

Back at the senator's main property situated between the two farms, Julia has a side wing of the house, she invites Marcus to join her.

She leaves the lights off in her bedroom. He sits back on a chair, and she enters the room wearing a silk veil with the moonlight coming in through the window.

Julia moves closer to him and becomes more provocative. He can smell her eastern perfume as she swirls closer, touching his legs with her new scarves. She starts to dance to the music, which can be hear from the continuing party cerebrations close to the bonfire some distance away.

'I am trying to do the dance of the seven veils – why are you just lying there ignoring me?'

'I've had a tiring day.'

'Well you seemed all right earlier in the day.'

'That was before your father spoke with me.'

'Are you going to blame your misery on my father?'

'Well, yes!'

She looks outside, 'Come quick and look out of the window.'

Marcus looks out and sees Quintus, and his two best friends, pretending to be horses and jumping over logs as they make their way to the main house. Across each of their shoulders are long streamers of ribbons, at the other end of the ribbons three women are each holding as if they are reigns, pretending they are charioteers.

They are laughing and jumping and occasionally putting arms around each other. Everyone making merriment with a little help from too many glasses of wine.

Marcus does not recognise the women holding the senator's ribbon-reins, which Quintus holds over his left-shoulder, but notices that she is tall, slim and an attractive woman in her mid-forties. She looks a little like Crispus' wife – surely not!

'What is your father doing with Crispus' wife?'

'Oh, my father and Livia have been good friends for some years. She is here especially for the war game. Livia is the twin sister of Crispus' wife.

'My father has a heated pool and every year they all head there before changing into warm clothes and then they sit by a huge fire.'

She turns to him, 'Please don't just sit there feeling miserable – let's enjoy the end of a long weekend, and also have fun.'

It was not the time, he thought, to bring up the conversation her father had with him.

He moved onto the bed totally exhausted, and before dropping off to sleep saying, 'You look beautiful – tomorrow I will make it up to you.'

But he is annoyed with Julia's father for telling his friends, the consul and Dio, that he was going to fight as *Achilles* to see if his daughter's boyfriend would be able to stand up to him acting at *Hector* in a fight. Surely the man does not need to fight before he can make an assessment him, and have his friends rallying around as if in a gladiatorial contest.

Quintus had the opportunity of inviting him around to talk about their journey to and from Capri, but instead chose to mention the letter received from his friends in Terracina and that contents of the letter had been intercepted by Gundher. He chose the time of the fight to disclose this news, and there was no need for Quintus to mention Gundher.

Just as he was closing his eyes he recalled *Achilles*' meeting with king *Priam*. Each man must earn respect, and obviously, this is the way it must be between himself and Julia's father – both finding respect for the other.

CHAPTER TWELVE

December - Hedonism and Friends

Crispus' wife sends a message to Julia to come to her new home, mid-morning, as she would like to discuss a choice of statues to be placed around her swimming pools.

One pool is small, which is heated, and the water only reaches her waist. The other pool is much larger and has a shallow and a deep end.

Besides wishing to have some statues, she would also like ideas for the seating, and outdoor lamps, and tables. I want you to organise everything – don't worry about the cost, and I will leave it to your good taste. She signed the note Portia.

Julia still had the problems with Crispus, but had met his wife on several casual occasions, and remembers her as a pleasant but quiet woman.

As she leaves the showroom she accidentally sees Crispus, when crossing a busy road, but decides not to mention Portia's note.

He is thinking about how to acquire an air of authority, and impress people with his new-found wealth.

'So pleased to see you here.' He looks around to see if enough people could see him and spoke in a loud voice for everyone in the road to turn to his bellowing.

'I gather that you are wanting some money?' Making it sound as if she were poor and needed a loan from him.

Slowly he takes the money out of his bag, and hands it to her slowly in dribs and drabs – turning to see if everyone is watching and counting. 'I am sure that having this money makes your life happier!' Making it seem that she was a pauper taking money from him.

He hurries away before she could provide an appropriate reply.

She wonders how Portia can put up with him.

Arriving at the new house the servant leads her into the atrium and says that she will tell the madam.

Soon the servant is back and says: "Madam is having a massage before her morning swim, but she asks me to bring you to her.'

Portia is an attractive woman in her mid-forties, tall and slender. Julia reckons that it must have been an arranged marriage by Portia's father, because any woman in her right mind would not have chosen Crispus.

Portia is lying on a massage bed, with a tiny piece of towelling covering her body, and a handsome looking male, about half Portia's age, massaging her.

Julia had never been massaged but it seems sensuous.

'Ignore Gaius, my massager, he looks after my body. My life these days is about keeping healthy and fit.'

Then she whispered to Julia, 'He's a eunuch so he is not interested in women.'

Julia thought that she would suggest to Marcus, as she has not yet told him what present she wishes to have from him, to celebrate the

Saturnalia, that she will have a massager to look after her body.

Whilst Portia is being massaged, she tells Julia about all the work she would like around her swimming pool.

'Let me show you,' and she sat up on the bed and then, with support from Gaius, she walked naked to the small pool.

Julia's eyes were now wide open. Not only looking at Portia's great figure, but as the three of them walk to the pool area, Julia tries hard to appear unabashed, and realises that she is the only one fully clothed.

Gaius, is was wearing an apron-type thigh cover, like those Julia had seen in Egyptian paintings, which he removes to prevent it getting wet in the pool.

He helps Portia into the heated pool and tells her to relax as he supports her by holding one hand under her stomach, and his other hand supporting her chin. She lies parallel with the top of the water. He instructs her to move her arms and legs as if she were a frog. They both moved in a circle around the shallow pool.

Julia is not sure whether Portia can swim or whether she just enjoys being supported.

Wandering around the pool area, Julia notices that the mosaic work has geometric patterns with tiles of tiny *tesserae* in blues and creams, and an occasional beige design of dolphins. Julia was thinking that she could expand on the dolphin idea around other parts of the pool area which is surrounded by a walled garden.

When she looks back at the pool, Portia has moved position and is lying on her back in the water. With her head stretch back, and chest raised up, she slightly moving her arms gently at her sides – attempting to keep herself afloat. Gaius is standing close at her side with one arm under her back.

As her nipples begin to protrude on the top of the water – Julia who tries not to notice – but is suddenly distracted by was seemed like an astronomical phenomenon taking place before her eyes – it seems as if it were a sun pillar, or a phoenix. Then her reasoning brings her to the conclusion that Gaius is not exactly a eunuch.

Upon returning to the showroom she decides that her new customer will probably prefer a statue of *Eros* at one end of the pool and a statue of *Apollo* by at the other end.

A few days later she returns with Gundher to take some measurements and designs. Portia had left her a message to say that she will not be there that day but the servant can let her in when she arrives in the morning.

There was no sign of the Gaius. Crispus' male slave, wearing a short tunic that the master had provided for winter and summer, let them in. It was a chilly December morning and he has been on his hands and knees trying to wash the mosaic floors in the entrance hall. Crispus had refused to take on the servants from the previous owner of the house – preferring to economise.

The slave has a lot of work to complete. In the summer months he takes all the smaller furniture outside, and quickly sweeps and washes the floor. In winter he moves the furniture from around different areas of the room whilst he cleans.

On this particular morning Crispus prevents him from completing his tasks because as he washes an area, Crispus walks over it, and keeps repeating this action as he mutters to himself. Not only does this action annoy the slave, but the master refuses to buy him a new tunic. He has worn the same one for two years, and hopes that as it is December he will receive a new one, but knows that the master will want to take the old one off him in exchange. There is no joy for him this Saturnalia.

Crispus did not even notice the servant, he was talking to himself about his visit to his banker to see if monies from his father's farm has arrived in his account.

*

Mid-December and the time of the Winter Solstice.

It is now the seventeenth of December, and Papinus is taking Anna and Rufus to the gathering at the Temple of Saturn on Capitoline Hill, close to the arch of Septimius Severus.

The temple also holds the State Treasury, being the taxes and other monies collected from state provinces, as well as taxes in Italy for water and sewage, taxes on land and manumission of slaves – all controlled by the senate with the emperor having overall power.

As they look at the temple, Papinus explains, 'The temple was built around BC 500 but was rebuilt in 42 by the senate. It is named after the Greek god *Cronos* (*Saturn*) who was associated with the harvesting of crops and shown as holding a scythe.

'*Chronus* (the god of Time who devoured all his children) seemed to be different from the Utopian Age Greek god Honia (*Cronus*) – a time when there were no rules or laws – an imagined Utopia. This god celebrates the harvest at the end of the season, and a time when rich and poor were equal.

Romans can enjoy these celebrations, and slaves can have time to relax and take part in the festivities. Everyone enjoys eating good food, play board games and sharing music together.'

Papinus moves closer, as the crowds gather around the area of the temple. He continues telling Rufus and Anna the history.

'In the temple is *Saturn*'s statue – *Saturn* being the Roman name for the god *Cronos* – which is sculpted from ivory and depicts an old man who is bent with age. His feet are bound with strips of fabric. These are removed each seventeenth day of December and over the years the god became equated with slaves who could be released from their chattels and treated as equals, even though this special occasion will be temporary.

'Everyone is supposed to find happiness, buy presents for family and friends, wear paper hats if they wish, and have feasts.'

Anna and Rufus watched dignitaries and senior officials who are part of the procession as the statue is brought from the *cella* for the procession and later they will feast with the god who is presented as a guest of honour.

'During this time slaves are free to wear their own choice of clothing, be exempt from punishment, and there is supposed to be no work,' explains Papinus.

'They can entertain their friends and sometimes use the opportunity, if their employer is around, to have him serve them their food. Some take the opportunity to point out their master's weakness and a slave's superiority.'

Rufus comments, 'I don't think that too many employers are happy to have their staff taking over the household and becoming abusive.'

'You are quite right, some slaves can get out of hand, which probably explains why several employers go and visit friends, or find a quiet spot, such as their study to hide in order to find more peaceful activities.'

After the official ceremony had taken place, Papinus walks with his friends around the tables where groups of people are playing music from their own countries and singing and dancing and eating their favourite specialities, and trying to recall the time when they were not part of Rome but in their own home land.

They talk with several groups who are wearing paper hats, giving presents to each other and laughing. They all make Papinus, Anna and Rufus welcome.

Papinus tells his friends, 'The Golden Age is a time when plants grew without toil, shepherds lazily watched their sheep, and people did not work ... an illusionary idealism. Some say that people never grew old – but then came the Silver Age and wealth, then the Bronze Age with weapons. The Iron Age brought lack of trust, hard work, and violence – but all these changes are inevitable as mankind needs to advance in knowledge'

*

Hoax or Deception

The senator, the consul, and Dio, are discussing whether Elagabalus' mother Soaemias, and grandmother, had created a hoax by dressing the boy to look like his uncle Caracalla. Their intention may have been for the two women to obtain power in Rome and get access to property, wealth and status.

'Firstly, when Caracalla died, the monies and properties from his estate, should have gone to his mother, Julia Domna. But before this could take place, she died. The next of kin being Elagabalus' grandmother, Julia Maesa, the sister of Julia Domna,' said the consul.

Dio agrees. 'Grandma would have all of Caracalla's estate and Julia Domna's estate to control.

'Elagabalus' real father, Sextus Varius Marcellus, died about two years before Elagabalus rose in position. Marcellus' Will and Estate, could have left Elagabalus and his mother with all his assets, but there has been no mention of Elagabalus being a wealthy or propertied young man.

'Macrinus, who became emperor after the assassination of Caracalla, but who only ruled for one year, should have been entitled to the inheritance of property from the previous empirical ruler, being Caracalla. Imperial inheritance being passed down from emperor to emperor.

'But it seems hardly likely that Macrinus would have had time to go through all the moneys received from provinces which came under the control of the emperor. Senators are not privy to this information.'

The consul comments, 'Sextus Varius Marcellus could possibly have told his wife, Soaemias about the type of work he had undertaken, and there is the possibility she talked about this to her mother, grandma Maesa, about the provinces with no two being alike in their finances in the way they were run or operated.

'Marcellus' work, on behalf of the emperor Septimius Severus and then his son, Caracalla, entailed the taxation of the provinces under the control of the emperor, also the emperor's *fiscus* or purse, which was also recovered in taxes and profits from mines and other businesses in the provinces throughout the Roman world, and the *res privatae* which relates to the emperor's inheritance of private estates and properties. Such properties either bequeathed to the emperor or by means of wealthy men who had lost most of their wealth – or property removed from wealthy people who were assassinated, on the orders of the emperor, would mainly have gone to the emperor's estate.'

'So it seems from what you say,' remarks the senator, 'that when Macrinus became emperor, the grandmother needed to act fast in order to keep the Severus monies within reach of her family, and that is why they made every effort to remove Macrinus, and his son whom he had made heir, but died around the time his father died.'

The consul asks if he can go into the kitchen and collect some items. Upon returning, he looks across at Dio and the senator, who sit opposite sharing a couch. They watch the consul as he places his pile of items from the kitchen at the side of him.

'Now, I am going to give you a demonstration of what Elagabalus' mother and grandmother may have known about Roman finances.

'On your side of the table you are the senators of Rome and on my side of the table you can imagine me as the emperor.'

He places on the table thirty fruit tarts. 'There are roughly thirty provinces. These are made up of the old provinces, being roughly one-third, are from the time of the Roman Republic, such as France, Greece, and so on, at the time of Julius Caesar, which are your provinces coming under the senate's control. Under which you control those legions and expenses and retrieve any profits from taxes and customs and so on.

'I will give you ten fruit tarts and these, which are so-called moneys received, will go into your *aerarium* or the state treasury, which is in the Temple of Saturn, which helps to support Rome.

'Just remember, the emperor has overall control of the senate.

'I will take the twenty tarts – which relate to the two-third provinces that were obtained after Julius Caesar, or when the Roman Empire was created by Augustus. Of course, these wealthy provinces include those that have gold, silver and tin mines and other minerals. These provinces stretch from Asia-Minor across Europe to Britain, and North Africa, and the Mediterranean countries such as Syria and joining up with Egypt.

'So I benefit with twenty fruit pies. Which I shall place in front of me, being the emperor.

'All customs duty, fishing right fees, incomes received from taxes paid by the people in these lands, after expenses comes to me. As benefits, I will take 20 figs from the pile. Of course, I use auxiliary forces in many of these countries which lessens the expenses on Roman legions, and these are paid for by those countries, but I have the military strength from these auxiliaries should I wish to strengthen my forces elsewhere.

'This in turn means that I not only have control over all the legions in the 20 provinces mentioned, I also have control over all the auxiliaries. In other words, should the senators decide to overthrow me, they do not have sufficient legions under the control of the senate.

'Therefore, all the moneys from the provinces goes into the emperor's or imperial account, the *fiscus*. The senators have no access or information on the running of the provinces, and each province has a different set of rules.

'There is also the emperor's purse, *res privata,* which is land or property inherited from previous emperors – so some nuts for me.

'I have also forgotten that if someone dies without leaving a Will or heir, or if I as imaginary emperor have anyone killed, I inherit the man's estate, or if I send someone into exile, I can inherit part of the estate. So that leaves me with biscuits and cakes.'

The two men at the other end of the table decide to stop the consul before there is nothing left for them to eat in the kitchen.

'You forgot to give us our ten figs. Now we can see why you enjoy being a consul over a province!'

The senator says jokingly, 'I think I must check the wine store just in case you have been adding too much of wine and less water to the glasses, as your mind is working overtime.'

'Let's get back to your premise about whether the grandmother created a hoax or a deception,' said Dio.

'Septimius Severus gave Caracalla the name of Antoninus, linking him with the earlier emperor's estates.

After Caracalla's death, a year later Elagabalus upon being declared emperor, also took the same name Antoninus. Therefore, Elagabalus, legitimately or illegitimately, is entitled to estates of previous emperors, such as empirical land and buildings.

'I think that by using Elagabalus as Caracalla's son, all these estates will be inherited by

Elagabalus. Most of all, making his grandmother exceedingly powerful.

'It seems to me that this is where the deception lies, because the grandmother may well have been aware of this financial gain. Elagabalus was just a naïve tool or ploy in the game of wealth.'

'It's an interesting argument, but I'd prefer to discuss the wine in front of me,' remarks Dio.

The senator fills up everyone's glass. The wine glasses are on long stems and the rims of the glasses are coloured red and gold, showing the noble art of workmanship of Italian glassblowers.

'Give me your comments on this particular wine?'

Dio replies, 'Well the glass receptacle is an excellent choice. I wonder whether Epicurus was right about one person's interpretation of taste. I find this wine being smooth to the taste, clear deep red in colour, more dense than the previous wine, and with a smell of the flowers, such as lavender, grown in the vicinity of the vineyard.'

'As far as I'm concerned,' responds the consul – 'Epicurus was arguing, if I recall, on whether what I perceive is the same as what you perceive. I could interpret the wine as warm to hot, I have never heard of the flowers mentioned in the field and can't even imagine them, and see the red as medium to light.'

'Well let's drink some different wines and see whether we agree or disagree on a few more – I really like discussing these perceptions.'

Each new wine they would toast 'Here's to Epicurus and his little atoms.'

They keep adding water to the wine, but as the hours progressed it became difficult to know how much water there was in proportion to the alcohol level of the wine.

One of the men mutters, 'Perhaps water quantities should be the next point of discussion.'

But they all drop off to sleep before the discussion every happens.

*

Celebrating the Saturnalia, Lucy and Petrus have gone to stay with his parents on the coast. Ndio receives presents from the family and even Rufus has given her a bracelet made from silver with her two names, Ndio and Safiya the name which her African friends have given her. When the showroom is closed, she makes a visit all her friends and they exchange gifts.

Gundher is left to supervise a huge meal for the staff and small gifts of biscuits and jams and small dolls or toys for their children. He does not allow them to get drunk and ruin the house and furniture, so makes sure that they were only entertained in the garden or atrium.

*

Are servants more intelligent than their masters?

Sextus, wraps a cape around his shoulders to keep warm whilst sitting on one of the benches in his garden by the pond viewing the goddess *Diana* and the beautiful lighting from the sky behind her. His little dog, named after Queen Dido of Carthage, the mythical queen who had fallen in love with the ancient *Aeneas* when was travelling to Rome from Troy at the end of the Trojan War, is a fluffy puppy which had been given to Sextus by Marcus. Little Dido had wandered off.

As he glances around he notices his head servant from the house creep behind the carved wooden deer of *Acteon*. Sextus knew that it was the time of the year when they expect some presents.

Pretending to be the deer talking, the servant says. 'I know that I am cleverer than my master.'

Sextus replies: 'Well, *Acteon*, if you are so clever you would not have been turned into a stag.'

The hidden slave replies: 'It's not so much as to whether one is a stag or not a stag – or whether one is *Acteon*, or not *Acteon* - but whether servants are cleverer than their masters'.

'Give me an example?'

'I only need to sip the remnants of wine from a near empty amphora container to tell if it's a good or a bad wine.'

Rather sarcastically, since Sextus purchases all the wine, he replies, 'How unbelievably clever of you!' But the sarcasm misses its mark.

'Seems that I have wasting my years going to vineyards, looking at lavender and herbs planted nearby to understand whether the flavours have influenced the taste of wines – and questioning whether my palate can detect soils and countries where the grapes are grown, and how much rain there was that particular year.

'Why, instead of going to different types of vineyards whether in eastern France, Italy, Greece, or other places, I could have just taken an amphora of wine in the storeroom and if the taste seemed sour like vinegar or unpleasant, I could have thrown it away. It is phenomenal – you – an expert taster!

'Just to think that I have gone to so much trouble to buy expensive wines for my friends who are connoisseurs – and after our dining and the remnants go into the kitchen – you, with your expertise, can tell if it's a good or bad year!

'Well, *Acteon* – the man, or deer, or stag – I should point out that I have left half of an amphora of wine for my head servant to enjoy with his friends. Whether I have given him a good wine or not – he will be clever enough to judge!'

With that, the figure behind the carved stag disappears rather hurriedly away.

*

Imaginative thoughts

Dido has reappeared. She was wandering behind leaves, and exploring the garden paths, and upon returning to Sextus the little puppy notices his laces and finds fun in tugging at them, testing and chewing. Then she gives a little bark of joy.

It is growing cold when Papinus joins him in the garden.

'I hope you are planning to go indoors so that we can sit by a huge fire – it's getting quite chilly in the garden.'

They move to a guest cottage in the grounds that has a large sitting area, two bedrooms, small kitchenette, and bathroom facilities. They will not have any disturbance from the servants wanting to enjoy the Saturnalia, feasting and drinking.

At this time of the year Sextus and a few close friends, sit back and enjoy talking about a chosen ancient Greek satire. This year they have chosen Aristophanes' play, *The Birds,* written in BC 414. But it has more depth than just being about birds.

Aristophanes' satire points a finger at the Athens, which at that time was increasing its power over Greek islands that were being forced to pay tribute to Athens and support its control over the Delian League.

The island Melos, an independent island, wished to remain neutral, but Athens called upon it to pay tribute with Athens threatening to destroy the lives of those on the island if they do not agree to acquiesce.

Athens had the island surrounded and the islanders starved, then the city was taken, men killed, and women and children became slaves.

Aristophanes play is about birds that create a cuckoocloudland, and the gods are having problems because humans are not supporting them, and the birds with their Utopia in the sky start being supported by humans.

Eventually the birds become more powerful and start building walls around their cuckoocloudland, removing human freedom, making laws, and become tyrannical.

Eventually the gods return the birds to their natural ways, and peace once again retained.

The comedy is about two men with a pet crow and a pet jackdaw, and this increases with people becoming a nightingale, a hoopoe, and a swallow.

Aristophanes, with his satire, is showing that Athens, like the birds, was becoming too controlling with its laws and finance and ignoring the true spirit of kinship.

Sextus and Papinus have much to discuss with wars and reality and gods and imagery. But they also decide to compare it with the Trojan War story told around several hundred years earlier. In those early years Greeks all supported one another, there was a common respect among leaders on opposing sides for burying their dead. If Agamemnon had left the fight to return home, there would be little retribution. Or if Achilles had decided to return to be with his father, nobody would have stopped him, but these men all recognised that kinship and the community mattered to them and they support it at all cost.

All the Achaean/Greeks act honourably as one, and were like a large family. The Trojans had similar principles.

Sextus and Papinus are determined to enjoy their evening, discussing Aristophanes satires and not looking too deeply into his imaginative humour, but accepting his writings as an alternative to the problems of ancient Greek political life.

They also want to discuss Homer's insight into weapons and inventions used in the Trojan War. A Symposium on alternative thinking.

*

Fabius, Rufus and Anna make their way to Sextus house as invited guests and are prepared to give their views on 'fantastical inventions' as Fabius likes to call them.

Fabius wishes to discuss the ancient Greek, Ctesibius, (BC 285-222) of Alexandria, who invented a piston pump using a system of compressed air.

On the way, they speak about the Trojan War party, and Anna gives her views on the gods.

'I am amazed at *Hephaestus* making a helmet that flashes out fire. It is pretty scary stuff.'

'But the joy was all is *Diomedes* who wears the helmet and the visor,' says Rufus.

'I agree,' comments Fabius. 'Homer takes us into a marvellous world of gadgets and contraptions that can self-operate. In Rome we might build beautiful buildings, but we do not have the imagination of the ancient Greeks. In those very early years of the bronze and iron age we can read about people dreaming about automatons which could move by themselves.'

'Well, Homer also related the tale of an automaton named *Talos*. It was supposed to be able to patrol the island of Crete, walking around it three times a day, to protect it from pirates,' comments Rufus.

'The interesting thing is that Homer's *Talos* is written much earlier than Ctesibius' invention.

Therefore, one wonders how the automaton managed to walk' said Fabius.

Anna knows very little about Greek history and the mythical gods, but does not want to be left out of the conversation.

'The way I see it – ancient Greeks pass these images on for future builders of automatons to improve upon their ideas.'

She is silent for a few minutes, 'I am imagining myself being on the island of Crete, with its beautiful shoreline, watching the waves, listening to the birds overhead in the trees, and looking at wild plants – a paradise. Suddenly, I perceive Homer's *Talos* walking towards me. I can't think which scares me the most – a *Talos* or being attacked by pirates.'

They all gave thought to being on the island. One or two believe that it would be exciting to see pirates, and others saw a future in having protection by a *Talos*.

'But on reflection - how would a *Talos* differentiate between a pirate, and a person who is a resident of the island of Crete,' says Rufus.

'That is beyond our wildest Roman dreams ... a world of fantasy, and Homer at his best ... just enjoy,' remarks Fabius.

*

Nostalgia and futuristic anticipation

Marcus is by the pond checking that all the lanterns have been lit. There is a cupboard behind the fountain where the water in front of the statue of Diana can occasionally thrust out. He had earlier asked the servant to put towels in there – he did not want people who visit to get their clothing wet and having to walk back to the house to dry themselves.

'I have decided what you can get me for a Saturnalia present,' says Julia.

'Well I have already bought you a small present, but tell me what you would really like to have.'

'I have decided upon a eunuch, preferably one who is not fully true eunuch, who can massage me and teach me to swim whilst I lie back naked, and gain good posture.'

'Where on earth did you get that idea?'

'Portia.'

Marcus found it extremely funny trying to imagine the scene.

'So, you want a eunuch, who can give you a massage and can help you swim?' With that he lifts her off the bench and jumps in the pool with her.

'I have just put on my make-up for the evening, and spent hours on my hair.'

They start fighting about in the water – but in a playful way.

Eventually he lifts her out over his shoulder as she was trying to kick and pound her arms on his back.

He lay her down on the grass – grabbed a towel out of the cupboard. 'Now tell me about the eunuch. And no, you are not having one as your present.'

Julia tells him about her visit to Portia. He can barely stop laughing.

'I am not going to buy you a eunuch so you can be like Portia, but I am quite happy to play at being the masseur. But I will need some instructions.'

'We can go to my bedroom. Sextus and everyone are all spending the evening in the guest cottage.'

As they make their way to his bedroom, he says, 'I remember the first time I saw you in my bedroom. I woke up, and saw a scary beast with black eyes and hair all over the face and looking like a monster, lying next to me!'

She interrupts. 'What you are saying to me is that you awoke early one morning – saw a beast with black eyes and hair all over the face – it must have been you looking at yourself in the mirror!'

Before he could speak she says, 'Oh by the way, I have brought with me the magic embroidered breast band that *Hera* wore, which *Hera* she borrowed from *Aphrodite*. I shall put it on but only after you make a promise.

'You must sit in this chair, and place your hands, forearms and elbows on the armrest. Only move when I give the instructions.'

'I promise,' he replies not knowing what the consequences will be if he breaks the promise.

'You must promise not to touch the magic breast band, which holds the magic, but you have to wear a blindfold – otherwise the realm of mystery will not work.'

'Just sit here whilst I put on my breast band, but no peeping through the blindfold,' with that she covers his eyes and goes out of the room.'

Like *Hera* she combs and loosens her hair so that it flows down just below her shoulders, oils and perfumes her body, like *Hera*, and returns to the room and removes her silk robe. He can hear the rustle of silk.

With his eyes closed he could feel the robe brush against his legs. After a few minutes, he can hear her moving across the room then back again.

As she comes closer to him she leans on him to test that the blindfold is firmly in place. But with that movement he can feel her oiled body brush up against his arms and realises that she is now naked except for her imaginary breast band that was supposed to have a thin strip of protective magic material across.

He can smell perfume in her hair and was desirous to see the breast band. Her body gently leaning close at times was too much for his imagination and his senses were roused.

'And now you can taste the nectar from the gods.'

He can taste a small amount of honey.

As she begins to gently rub oils on his arms and torso he feels her soft body rubbing gently against his bare legs, and at times his arms and chest. He is still wearing his towel after being in the pond – and he is now ready to rip off the blindfold.

He has a dilemma – should he break his promise to Julia and removing the blindfold and take control. After all, he is a full-blooded Roman. Or, should he just enjoy the stimulation of being enveloped in the illusion of *Hera* and the Greek myths.

He wonders – 'Now what would *Zeus* do!

21396232R00213

Printed in Great Britain
by Amazon